SHELTER FOR JERRICA

BLUEGRASS BRAVERY BOOK 5

DEANNDRA HALL

This book is a work of fiction. Names, characters, places, and incidents are products of the author's imagination or used fictitiously. Any resemblance to actual events or locales or persons living or dead is entirely coincidental.

Dear Readers,

Welcome to the Police and Fire: Operation Alpha Fan-Fiction world!

If you are new to this amazing world, in a nutshell the author wrote a story using one or more of my characters in it. Sometimes that character has a major role in the story, and other times they are only mentioned briefly. This is perfectly legal and allowable because they are going through Aces Press to publish the story.

This book is entirely the work of the author who wrote it. While I might have assisted with brainstorming and other ideas about which of my characters to use, I didn't have any part in the process or writing or editing the story.

I'm proud and excited that so many authors loved my characters enough that they wanted to write them into their own story. Thank you for supporting them, and me!

READ ON!

Xoxo

Susan Stoker

This book was inspired by the song

Drunk Girl as performed by Chris Janson.

May men everywhere become the man in that song and in this book.

CHAPTER 1

"Another one?"

Landon smiled at the girl wearing the standard-issue apron for the Blue Moon Bar. "Nah, but thanks."

"Come on and have another one, Hose! It's Saturday night, for fuck's sake!" Lucas "Stingray" Wilson taunted using Landon's nickname as he leaned against the bar and peered around Pete "Rodeo" Darnell and Hayes "Juice" Franklin to leer at Landon.

"Yeah, man, have another one. We're not ready to leave yet," Rodeo almost whined. "It's been a rough week."

They didn't have to tell Landon that. Everyone at their Taylorsville, Kentucky, firehouse had endured seven days of hell. Three of their own had been injured when the ceiling of the building where they were fighting a four-alarm had collapsed. And they'd lost two civilians when they couldn't reach a woman and her two-year-old son. Nothing hurt more than losing a child. But Landon had learned years earlier that trying to drown those images with alcohol got him nowhere except hungover and sick, not to mention poorer. "I think it's about time to go," he announced.

Sitting closest to him, Juice slapped him on the back. "You can't go yet! We haven't found you a girl!"

Oh, yeah. That's the very last thing on earth I need, he told himself. He loved his job, but every woman he'd dated had tried to talk him into doing something else. They didn't like being alone at night, didn't like the fact that his job was dangerous, wanted him to take something he'd make more money doing, or were somehow disappointed that he had feelings. That last one got him every time. Just because he fought fires for a living and had to be fearless in the face of danger didn't mean he was impervious to emotional hurt. As for fearless, he was scared shitless every time he answered a call. Danger lurked everywhere, and death was always at their door. All it took was one second and all the training in the world couldn't save a firefighter, and they all knew it.

"Uh-oh. There's a live bunch," Rodeo said and pointed.

On the other side of the room was a group of young women, and they were having a good time—a really, really good time. There were six of them, all various sizes, hair colorings, and features, but all in the same late twenties to mid-thirties age range. Five of them seemed very engaged, but a sixth one, a smaller woman who looked to be the oldest of the group, hung off to the side, sucking on something in an on-the-rocks glass. Landon's thoughts were interrupted when Juice said, "I'm going after at least one of them." With that, he stood and made his way across the room.

In three minutes, all five women were at the table, with the sixth still hanging back on the dance floor. "Who's your other friend there?" Landon asked the woman nearest him, a tall brunette.

"Oh, her? That's Jerrica. I don't think she wanted to be here," the girl answered.

"Why?"

"She's just not much of a socializer," another one of the young women answered, a striking African-American girl with beautiful teeth behind the most gorgeous smile Landon thought he'd ever seen.

"I see." As Landon watched, the woman sipped her drink, occasionally looking up and around almost as though she were checking on her friends, then stared back into the bottom of her glass.

God, they were drunk! One of the girls almost fell as she stood there, and two of the others grabbed her and righted her. Juice and Stingray were chatting them up, and from his seat on his stool, Rodeo had two girls cozied up, an arm around each of their waists. Stingray was doing the same, and Juice had one between him and the bar, his knee between her thighs as she stood there. One of the girls standing near Rodeo leaned over into Landon's personal space and stared right into his eyes, her breath heavy with liquor. "You're kinda quiet. I like that," she told him with an inebriated grin.

"Thanks."

"I like my men that way. No talking, just fucking. That's always best," she said. "My name's Jolie."

"Nice to meet you, Jolie," Landon said and reached out to shake her hand. Before he knew what was happening, she grabbed his hand and thrust it between her legs.

"Nice to meet you too, um, what did you say your name was?" she asked as he pulled his hand away from her.

"I didn't. You girls are having a good time, aren't you?" he asked, half mocking and half sarcastic.

"Yeah. All except Jerrica. She's kinda weird like that," the woman announced.

Landon had forgotten about her, and the young woman's comment made him turn. And what he saw terrified him.

Jerrica stood on the dance floor, drink still in her hand, swaying dangerously between two men. One had a hand on the outside of her thigh and as they danced, he lifted her dress higher and higher toward her hip. The other had his arms around her waist, inching his hands upward toward her breasts. But that wasn't the scary part.

The scary part was the fact that Jerrica's eyes were closed and he was pretty sure she was oblivious to everything going on around her. So drunk that she could barely stand, Landon knew if the men moved away, she'd just crumple to the floor. Her five friends kept chatting up his buddies, who were more than happy to oblige them in hopes of a conquest that night. They were paying no attention to her—none at all.

He reached into his back pocket to pull out his wallet and pay his bar tab when movement caught his eye and he turned just in time to watch the two men dance Jerrica to the edge of the dance floor and through a doorway that led to an emergency exit. The first thought in Landon's mind was his younger sister, Liella, and the aftermath of her attack when she was on spring break in Florida. The men who'd raped her had pulled her from a drunken crowd, unnoticed by any of her friends, and thrown her down behind a dumpster, where they'd taken turns with her as she fought and whimpered. He remembered the interviews with the police, how condescending they'd been toward his baby sister, how angry he'd been at their insistence there was nothing they could do, and how she'd suffered. She'd never been the same, and there was no way he was letting another woman go through that, no matter who she was. Not if he had anything to do with it.

The fifty he'd pulled from his wallet floated onto the bar's shiny surface and Landon headed directly toward the exit hallway, not giving a shit about his change. He could hear voices, male voices, and the sight that greeted him flooded adrenaline into his system.

They had the woman pinned to the wall. One had her dress up around her waist and was pulling her thong down, and the other had pulled down a strap on her dress and was working on unhooking her bra. Landon didn't think past the next ten seconds when he barked out, "What the fuck do you think you're doing?"

"Back off, motherfucker," one of the guys growled.

He pulled himself up to his entire six feet and four inches of height. "That's my baby sister. You'd better have a way to explain yourself or suffer the consequences. Your best bet is to just walk away and I'll try to forget this ever happened."

"Or you're gonna do what?" the other guy asked, twirling her thong in the air on his finger.

"I'm going back out here to get my three firefighter buddies and the four of us are going to tear you into quarters and feed you to the hogs down at the livestock yards. Is that what you want?" Landon asked in the most menacing tone he could muster, clenching and unclenching his fists the whole time.

The two guys looked at each other and shrugged. "Whatever the fuck. These drunk bitches are a dime a dozen," one answered. They dropped her thong and walked away, making sure to brush into Landon as they made their way back to the bar area.

When he turned back to Jerrica, she'd slid down the wall and was sitting on the floor, legs all akimbo and head down. "Jerrica? Jerrica, my name's Landon. Can you talk to me?" He was beginning to worry a little about alcohol poisoning until she finally lifted her head.

"I ga … I gotta … my keys …" she mumbled and reached for her clutch where it had landed about four feet away in the struggle. When she did, she simply fell over.

Oh, shit. Well, I guess I'm committed to taking care of this one, Landon told himself as he looked around. There was no one to help him, so he grabbed her clutch, then picked up her thong and stuffed it inside. Fortunately, he found her keys inside when he opened her clutch. Landon took them, closed the bag, then stepped outside the exit. One press of the button told him the red Pontiac G6 at the edge of the parking lot was hers, so he drove it up to the door, then left it running while he picked her up, carried her out, and strapped her into it.

He'd almost pulled out of the parking lot when he realized he had no idea where he was going, so he pulled over and parked. Luckily for him, her wallet was there and intact, and he found her address easily enough. It was an area he knew fairly well, and it was only ten minutes away.

The little car rolled to a stop in the driveway in front of her side of the duplex, and Landon unlocked the door and placed her clutch and keys on the counter, then went back for Jerrica. It was a bit of a struggle to get her out of the car, but once she was in his arms, he didn't stop for anything. He didn't even bother to close the front door as he carried her down the hallway and into the first room he came to.

Her bed was unmade, and he laid her gently on it, then went back outside and closed the car door, stepped back into the apartment, and set the lock on the car with her remote. Once he'd closed the front door, he went back to check on her.

As soon as he stepped into the room, he heard her whine, "I've gotta pee." *Well, hell, she's already not wearing any panties,* he told himself, so he carried her into the bathroom and set her on the toilet, careful to pull her dress up and out of the way.

She sat there, head down, until Landon said, "Jerrica, you're on the toilet. Go ahead, honey." He was rewarded with a sound that let him know she'd heard him, and when he'd helped her get cleaned up, he carried her back to the bed. Rummaging around in her dresser, he came up with a big tee shirt and a pair of bikini panties. After he'd slipped the panties onto her and pulled her dress off over her head, he dropped the tee onto her. But he was careful to sit behind her as he unhooked her bra and let it fall before pulling the tee shirt down. She didn't have much dignity left, and he'd decided he would give her all the dignity he could. As soon as he was finished, he turned her loose and she fell, ragdoll-like, onto the bed.

In a couple of minutes he'd covered her with the

sheet and lightweight blanket and she seemed to snuggle into her pillow. After switching off the little lamp beside the bed, he stepped out into the hallway and pulled the door closed. Back in the kitchen, he left a note beside her clutch that had nothing but his phone number on it, then turned on a lamp sitting on a side table next to what had to be her favorite chair, judging from the soft drink cans, magazine, and electronics remotes on the table's surface.

He opened the front door and surveyed his surroundings. The woman was home and safe, dressed for bed, and would hopefully wake with nothing more than a pounding headache the next day. Her clutch, complete with keys and wallet, were on the counter, and the car was locked up. With one last look down the hallway, Landon turned the button on the knob and stepped outside, pulling it shut behind him.

On the way there he'd noticed a convenience store about two blocks back, so he called a cab as he walked and asked them to meet him. They picked him up, took him back to pick up his truck, and twenty minutes later, Landon unlocked the door to his house and stepped inside, exhausted. All the way to the bedroom, while he brushed his teeth and hair and readied for bed, he cursed the fact that there'd been no one there for his sister when she'd needed them and blessed the universe that at least Jerrica hadn't met the same fate. He hadn't been a hero. He'd just done what any man would do in the same situation.

And he cursed again because he knew that wasn't true.

* * *

It was quiet, or so she thought, until she heard a bird chirping somewhere right outside the window. Her first attempt to open her eyes was rewarded with the sensation of her skull cracking open, so she closed them.

Another ten minutes passed and, little by little, she managed to open one lid. To her surprise, her surroundings looked familiar. When she got the other eye open, she realized she was in her own bed. That got her attention, and she sat straight up, only to have that blinding pain pierce her brain again.

Her hands wandered down her own length. She had on a tee shirt and panties. To top it off, the panties weren't the ones she'd been wearing the night before. How had that happened? And she didn't remember driving home. How she'd come to be in her own bed was yet another mystery. It took her a bit but after twenty minutes, she finally felt sturdy enough to stand.

The trip to the bathroom was agonizing, but she made it. From there, she headed up the hallway, a hand on either wall, until she got to the living room. The curtains were open, and the light was blinding. Stumbling to the kitchen, hanging onto furniture as she went, she managed to find her way to the coffee pot and start some. Thank god the coffee and filters were out on the counter! Her eyes closed as she stood and waited for the coffee to finish, and it wasn't until she'd poured a cup and taken half a dozen sips that she saw it.

Her clutch. She didn't remember having that either. When she opened it, her car keys were the first thing she saw. She pulled them out, and her thong fell out too. What the hell had happened the night before? Was her car there? She half ran, half staggered, to the door and looked out. Yep—it was there in the driveway. Had she driven herself home? Jerrica prayed she hadn't. At least her car looked fine. Apparently if she *had* driven, she'd made it home okay.

But when she turned back to her clutch, she saw it for the first time—a piece of paper with a phone number on it. *Oh, god, what did I do?* she asked herself. Had someone been there and left just before she woke? Had she ... She didn't want to think about it. After she finished her coffee and poured another cup, curiosity got the better of her, and she pulled out her phone—also still in her bag—and called the number.

It rang twice and a male voice answered, "Hello?"

She couldn't—she just couldn't. Jerrica hit END and dropped the phone on the counter. It no sooner hit the countertop than it started to ring.

The number she'd just called popped up on the screen, and Jerrica groaned as she picked it up and answered with a timid, "Hello?"

"Hi. Did you just call my number?"

No denying it now. "Um, yeah. I'm sorry. Must've been a wrong number," she stammered, embarrassed and terrified.

"Jerrica? Is that you?"

OH SHIT! What the hell did I do? her aching brain screamed. "Uh, yeah. It's me."

"Good. Are you okay?"

"Uh, yeah. I'm okay." She waited for a few seconds in silence, then asked, "Who is this?"

A soft chuckle came from the phone. "It doesn't matter. I just wanted to make sure you were okay. I was hoping you'd call so I wouldn't have to worry about you anymore."

Worry about her? Why would a stranger worry about her? "Do I know you?" she asked, still confused.

"No. And I don't really know you. But I took you home last night and left you. Do you remember what was happening?"

"No."

"Good. I'm glad. I didn't want something to happen to you, and I'm glad it didn't," the male voice said, and she was perplexed when she realized there was a quality to its tone that made her feel comfortable.

"Did we …" She tried, but she couldn't finish the sentence.

There was that chuckle again. "No. I drove you home, helped you into the bathroom, got you dressed for bed, and called a cab to take me home. No harm, no foul. But sweetie, please, next time, either go with friends who'll pay more attention to you, or don't go at all. You almost got yourself assaulted. And you need to watch that drinking too."

"What the hell? You're going to lecture me?" she almost yelled. The guy was nervy—she'd give him that.

"Yeah, says the man who kept you from being raped by two guys who were hellbent on doing exactly that," he said, his voice stern. "Just some friendly advice from a guy who might've gotten his ass kicked for taking care of you." The man was silent for a few seconds, then added, "You're welcome."

Jerrica's cheeks burned. "Yes. I'm sorry. Thank you. I appreciate it. You didn't have to do it, but you did, and I'm grateful." Who was this guy? And why did he even care? It didn't make sense. Then something popped into her mind. "Could I take you to lunch or something to thank you?"

"Not necessary. I'm just glad you're okay and that I was there to handle the situation. I wish somebody had been there for my … I'm just glad you're all right. Have a good day, Jerrica, and I hope you feel better later."

Before she could say another word, the phone went dead. She was a little insulted that he wouldn't even let her thank him properly. *Oh, well, he's either way, way too hot for me or such a dog that he figures I wouldn't give him the time of day*. She didn't know which it was, but there was one thing she knew for sure.

That voice was drop-dead sexy, and she really

wanted to meet the man behind it. Before she could forget, she went in, saved his number, and gave him the name *Sexy Voice*. Maybe someday she'd manage to track him down. Until then, he'd just be the thing dreams were made of.

* * *

"Where the fuck did you go last night?" Juice asked before Landon could even get his jacket out of his locker.

"Just went home," Landon answered, never looking at him.

"With the drunk girl?" Rodeo asked.

Landon shook his head. "No. I didn't go home with her."

"That's funny," Juice said with a grin. "Your truck was still in the parking lot, but you were nowhere to be found."

Landon didn't want to meet his eyes. He didn't want to talk about it. All the guys at the station teased him constantly. They just didn't understand, and they'd never understand because they didn't want to. "Yeah, well, I took a cab home because I'd had so much to drink."

"One of us could've taken you home," Stingray announced.

"You were worse off than I was in that department," he threw back. "Besides—"

"Oddly, that drunk girl disappeared the same time you did, Hose. What a coincidence, huh?" Rodeo said, laughing.

Landon went on with what he was doing, seething. Oh, they'd have a field day with him if they knew the whole story. He'd never hear the end of it. Fortunately for him, there were only three other people who knew what had happened. Two would never say a word, and the third didn't even know who he was. His secret was safe for the moment.

"Fox?" a booming voice called out.

"Coming, captain," Landon called back as he slammed his locker shut.

"Ohhhhh, what have you done now?" Rodeo droned, followed by a snicker.

"I'm sure something as equally shitty as the things you've done," Landon threw back with a sadistic grin. They loved tormenting him, and if he had a chance to sling it back, he would.

"Close the door," Captain Martin said as soon as he'd stepped into the small office. "Have a seat." Landon sat down, nervous as a long-tailed cat in a room full of rocking chairs. It was the moment of truth. "The city manager has looked over your paperwork and all the recommendations. I can't tell you this officially, but I've got it on good authority that your application for promotion is going through without a hitch." Landon breathed a sigh of relief. "I *can* tell you, in all the years I've put in with the department, I've never had another officer who's been as conscientious and dedicated as you, Fox. You do a good job and, more importantly, you care about people. It makes you extremely good at what you do. So congratulations, Lieutenant Fox."

Landon couldn't help himself—he jumped straight up out of his chair and blurted out, "Oh, god, thank you, Captain Martin! Thank you so much!"

"Say nothing, since it's not official yet," Martin cautioned him.

"Yes, sir. Thank you, sir. You won't regret it, I promise."

Captain Martin rose and extended his hand. "Please *don't* make me regret it, lieutenant!" he said with a laugh.

"Never, sir!" Landon shook his hand, gave him a small salute, and headed out the door, then spun around. "I'm so sorry! Did you want anything else, sir?"

"Yeah. Could you please make some of that vegetable soup this weekend? I love that stuff."

Landon laughed. "You've got it, captain! Thanks again." He headed back up the hallway and almost began to whistle, then thought better of it. The guys couldn't see him acting almost giddy. They'd want to know what was going on, and that wasn't something he could share just yet.

"Are we going out Friday night?" Stingray asked halfway through the day.

Landon shrugged. "I dunno. Doesn't make me any difference. You guys could come over and we could—"

"Stay in? Where's the fun in that? We need to go out! Find some girls!"

"Yeah, that worked well for you last night," Landon said. Then he noticed the room had gotten very, very quiet. Pivoting slowly, he looked at the three of them. They were all grinning. "Awww, you didn't ..."

"Let me just say, those two blonds know how it's done," Rodeo said with a grin.

"So did the brunette and the redhead," Stingray added.

Juice just smiled. "I doubt any pair of them was any better than that sexy, dark beauty I took home with me." Landon just shook his head until Juice said, "And I guess you're going to tell us you didn't tap that blond you took home."

"I told you, I didn't—"

"Right, right. Whatever," Stingray said just as the tone went off.

"Station Two, Station Two," the dispatcher called over the loudspeaker, "first responders and all personnel. Respond to structure fire, four ten Broadway. Reported to be empty and fully engulfed."

"Here we go," Rodeo yelled as he pulled on his gear. In less than two minutes, they were on their way, sirens blaring, with the first responder bus streaking away in front of them. Radio chatter told them Stations One and Four were also responding, and Landon knew Station Three was on standby if they were needed.

The building was indeed fully engulfed, with flames shooting up thirty feet into the air. Before they could even get out of the truck, the second floor collapsed into the lower part of the building, sending ash and sparks everywhere. When the truck from Station Four pulled up, Landon yelled to their commander, "Building to the east! Prepare for spread and hose 'er down!"

"Got it!" their lieutenant, Carey Bentley, yelled back.

Landon and his men prepared to enter the back of the structure, aware that it might not be possible. As soon as the door was pried open, they were met with a surge of flames, and he knew it was too dangerous. By the time they had hoses trained on it and were pouring the opening full of water, Station One's ladder truck had arrived and their officers were above the inferno and spraying down into it.

Four hours later, the two-story building with a twenty-four-hundred-square-foot footprint on a corner in the downtown business district was reduced to a pile of smoldering rubble. Thanks to Station Four's help, the building beside it was intact save for a bit of water damage. Seeing as how it was a mechanic's shop, that was probably no big deal for them. The lot would be unsellable, and it would be razed and sit there in the depressed little downtown area forever. For that,

Landon was truly sad, but there was nothing to be done except clean up the debris.

And he knew when the city put out a plea for residents to help clean it up, he'd be right there in the middle of it, moving charred timbers and shoveling up cinders. That was who he was and what he did. Everything in his past had prepared him to be a servant.

And it was all he'd ever dreamed it would be.

* * *

It was all she could do to drag herself to work, and even harder to keep going. There was a patient to be transferred to ICU who lost control of his bowel functions every ten minutes, and they'd spent the early part of the evening cleaning him up over and over again. She'd be glad when he went on upstairs and it was their problem, not the emergency room's responsibility. With the lingering headache and the upheaval in her stomach, the odor made her positively green.

And the ER nurse's station had heard the transmissions from the fire department but, thankfully, no one had been injured. The only other situation they'd seen was an overdose brought in by a police officer. One look told them it was almost too late, and they'd managed to save the kid's life, but he'd be forever impaired by his decision to shoot up tainted heroin.

Impaired by his decision. Jerrica knew that could've been her the night before if it hadn't been for the mystery man, as she'd come to think of him. Her break was almost over when she made a decision she hoped she wouldn't regret. Hands shaking, she took out her phone, found the contact, and touched her fingertip to it. It rang twice before that same voice said, "Hello?"

"Hi, um, I don't know what to call you."

There was a laugh on the other end. "You don't have to call me anything."

"How 'bout I just call you Superman?" she asked with a giggle.

"Oh, I'm a lot of things, but a man of steel I'm not." Then the phone fell silent.

Jerrica was stuck. What was she supposed to say? Then she remembered. "Uh, um, I just wanted to thank you again. I saw this boy who overdosed on heroin, and he's alive, but he has severe brain damage and he'll never be anything that passes for normal again. That could've been me last night."

"Especially if you'd planted that little G6 into a tree," he scolded.

"Exactly. So I wanted to say thanks one more time and I won't ever do anything like that again. I promise." Fishing in her brain, she couldn't come up with anything else to say.

"Good. Well, you take care of yourself." Once again, the silence was awkward, but Jerrica didn't want to stop talking to him. His voice was soothing, and she needed that.

"Um, okay. Well, thanks again. And is it okay if I call

you again sometime?" she asked, terrified of what he'd say.

"I've got a better idea. How 'bout I call you sometime?" he asked, and she had to wonder ... Was he interested in knowing her? Or was he blowing her off?

"Oh, yeah, right. I'll never hear from you," she said, knowing she sounded like a loser, just like she felt.

"You never know. Bye, Jerrica. Talk to you another time," he said.

"Yeah, okay. Bye, um, whoever you are," she answered and listened to him chuckle yet again before he hung up.

She sat there, phone in her hand, hoping her wetness hadn't soaked through her scrub pants. God, the man's voice was beyond sexy. The more she heard it, the more she wanted to know who he was.

CHAPTER 2

"Hey, Jerrica, want to go for a drink after work?" Mina called out to her as she stepped out of the nurses' lounge.

"No, I don't think …" *Wait!* her mind squealed with excitement. *If you go back to the same bar, you might see him! But how will you know if it's him? Don't overthink this, Jerrica,* she told herself. "Yeah. Sure. Why not? Meet you in the lounge after shift?"

"Yep. I'll be there. I'll ask the others. See ya later," Mina called to her as she stepped into the elevator to go back up to the urology floor. It was all Jerrica could do to keep from laughing as she thought about her friend spending her days catheterizing old guys' penises. What a fun job. Made her glad to be an ER nurse!

The early evening dragged on and ten o'clock couldn't come soon enough. She finished her charting at five after ten and wondered if Mina had waited for her. Sure enough, when she stepped into the lounge, Mina and Brandy were there. "Took you long enough!"

"I had charting to do. Sorry. Are we ready?" she asked as she slipped off her scrubs and pulled on the little cotton dress she'd hung in her locker at the start of her shift.

"Yeah. I am. Let's go," Brandy said as they headed out.

"By the way, where are we going?" Jerrica asked, fingers crossed.

Mina shrugged. "I guess the same bar where we were last night? It's a nice place. Good looking guys. And those guys we met up with last night … It would be awesome if we hooked up with them again, huh?"

Brandy nodded with a big smile. "Oh, yeah. I mean, that guy I was with? Stingray? Lawd, he's a hunk."

"Yeah, Juice was too. And tonight Betsy, Megan, and Jolie aren't with us, so we'll have them all to ourselves," Mina pointed out.

Something suddenly flashed through Jerrica's mind. "Hey, by the way, did they say what they do for a living?"

"Yeah. They're firefighters with the city. And trust me, it's easy to see why. They've got some very, very big hoses," Mina said with a laugh.

"Yeah. Big hoses, and they know how to handle them," Brandy said and giggled.

Firefighters. Another question. "Were they *all* firefighters?"

There was a collective groan from the other two. "Dear god," Brandy huffed, "don't tell us you didn't even ask that guy what he did for a living." Jerrica shook her head.

Mina's mouth fell open. "Jerrica, did you even get his name?"

Jerrica could feel herself blushing. "No."

"Oh, god, you took a guy home with you, fucked him, and didn't even ask him his name? Girl, you're a bigger ho than the rest of us!" Brandy shrieked.

"I didn't sleep with him!" Jerrica barked back.

"Shhhh, you two!" Mina hissed, looking around the lobby of the hospital as they walked through. "And don't tell us you didn't sleep with him."

"I didn't! I swear!" Her cheeks burned and her mouth went dry. They all thought she'd bedded the guy. Honestly, the truth was far more embarrassing. Drunky McDrunkerson had been dragged home by a good Samaritan and put to bed like a six year old. That was about as embarrassing as it got, at least from where she stood.

The bar was quiet when they stepped inside, and one glance told her none of the guys from the night before were there. They'd no more than taken a seat when she heard a male voice yell, "Lucky! Beers all around! Well, hello, ladies!" They all turned to find Stingray standing there.

"Hey, Stingray! How's it goin'?" Brandy sang out.

Before he answered, he wandered up beside her and wrapped an arm around her waist. "Hey, little lady! What's goin' on?"

"We were just sitting here wondering if anybody would show up. And here you are!" Mina sang out. "Hey there, Juice!"

"Hey, babe," he answered and stepped up to her stool. "Anybody bought you a drink yet?"

"Nope."

"Then let me be the first! Lucky, give this beautiful girl whatever she wants," Juice ordered and grinned at Mina. "And look who the cat dragged in!"

Jerrica turned and came face to face with the fourth man. Even in just jeans and a tee he was a guy who looked like he'd stepped right out of a men's health and fashion magazine. Was it him? There was only one way to find out, so she greeted him with a quiet, "Hey, good evening."

His smile was incredible, all white and dazzling. "Good evening to you too, Jerrica." Yeah—that voice. It had the power to do her in and she knew it.

"Hi, um …"

"Landon." He extended a hand and she took it. "Good to see you again."

"You too," she almost whispered. Something about him made her knees go weak and her head spin. He was more man than she could ever remember being that close to, muscles everywhere and that shock of dark brown hair, but it was his quiet demeanor that slayed her. She wanted to sidle right up against him until she could lean into him, to have him tighten his arm around her shoulders until she was pulled in close. The idea made her feel a bit lightheaded.

"Well, if that's not the most formal fuck-buddy greeting I've ever heard, I'm not sitting here!" Stingray brayed. "You could put a little passion into it!"

"Shut up, Stingray," Landon muttered.

"Gah, was it *that* bad?" Juice asked, his brows peaking and eyes wide. "Wow. How 'bout we leave you two lovebirds alone and let you go through your play-by-play until you figure out what went wrong? Ladies, let's retire to a booth, shall we?" Jerrica sat there, face burning, until the three men and her two friends had taken a booth across the room. It wasn't until then that she pivoted her head just enough to see Landon.

"Sorry about them," he said with a head toss toward the group. "They're convinced we, um, you know," he said, dropping his gaze to the beer bottle clasped in his hands, its amber bottom resting on the bar top.

"Yeah, that would've been horrible, huh?" Jerrica asked, her tone mocking.

"I didn't say that. But yeah, as gone as you were, it couldn't possibly have been good." She watched as he took another swallow of beer, his eyes scrutinizing the label on the bottle. "I'm just glad I was where I needed to be when I needed to be. You're safe. That's all that really matters."

"And thank you for that." Jerrica didn't know what else to say. The urge to hear that voice was gnawing at her, and there had to be a way to get him to talk to her. "When I spoke to you on the phone, I got the impression that's not the first time you've broken up something like … what was happening to me." And she waited.

It seemed to take forever for him to speak, and when he did, what he said pierced her heart. "Wish it wasn't. If I'd been in Florida when my baby sister …" He looked up at her and gave her a sad smile. "You know, *if* is a hard word to live with."

"I'm so sorry. Is she okay?"

"No." A deep sigh escaped his lips and she wished she'd never pushed. "I mean, physically, yeah. She's fine. But she's never been the same, and I don't think she ever will be. Being treated that way, only partially conscious and dragged behind a dumpster by two men, it did something to her mentally. Sometimes I get glimpses of the girl she used to be, but not often, and it seems like the longer it's been, the fewer and farther between those glimpses are." He took another swig of his beer and set the bottle down. "Liella is a beautiful woman, but she lives in a very fenced-in world in her mind now. And it's hard to see her that way."

Jerrica felt terrible. Her behavior the night before had taken him right back to a time that was unbearably painful for him. It was there on his face, all the hurt and regret, and she'd triggered that. "Landon, look, I'm sorry for the way I behaved last night. I started drinking and thinking, and that led to more drinking, and before I knew it, I was trashed. I won't ever make that mistake again. My god, those guys could've attacked you for standing up for me, and that would kill me."

"Nah. Should've seen their faces when I told them you were my baby sister and to leave you alone. The littlest of the two … I think his balls drew up into his belly and he'll never see them again!" Then he chuckled, and the sound was like music to Jerrica. Something about the guy struck a chord in her soul, and she realized what it was.

He was a good guy, one of the few left. Yeah, his buddies probably were too, but they were typical big-mouthed, get-your-groove-on guys. Not this one. There was something totally different about him, and she had to believe it was his raising, not just his personality. The smile she gave him was warm and genuine. "If you said something like that to me, I'd run for the hills!" she said and let out a little giggle.

"I'd never say something like that to you, but I *might* say, 'Jerrica, don't you think you've had enough to drink?' If there'd been somebody to say that to you, you wouldn't have been put in that position."

"But I was with my friends and …"

Landon shook his head, and it stopped her cold. "I realize that, and I'm not running them down, but you need to know that they weren't paying any attention to you. They were busy talking up my buddies and didn't even notice what was happening. I'm not saying you need new friends. But I *am* saying that if they're not going to pay attention to you, maybe you need to pay closer attention to yourself. Or maybe you need to run with some different friends. I dunno. None of my business. But if there's a next time—"

"There won't be," she assured him.

"But if there is, I probably won't be around to save you, and I don't want to think about what will happen." With that, he fell silent.

Jerrica scraped around in her head, trying to figure out what to talk to him about. "So, um, you guys work together?"

He nodded. "Yep. Fire and rescue. Out of Station Two." He leaned in and whispered, "They don't know it yet, but I'm being promoted to lieutenant."

Jerrica couldn't help but grin. "Congratulations! That's awesome!"

"Yeah, please don't tell your friends. They might let the cat out of the bag, and the captain asked that I keep it quiet until the city manager and the fire chief make the announcement."

"I won't say a word!" she promised. How to really engage him? "My last name is Ligon."

"I know. I had to look at your driver's license to know where you lived." He kept staring at his beer bottle. Getting him involved in the conversation was proving to be difficult.

"Oh, yeah." Nothing. So she decided to take a chance. "You have a last name, right?"

The way his eyebrows shot up almost made her laugh out loud. "Oh! Yeah! Um, Fox. My last name's Fox."

She wanted to say, *Now see? That wasn't so hard, was it?* but she didn't dare. "So what do you like to do in your spare time, Landon Fox?"

"I like to play video games."

"Yeah? My brother's big into gaming. He's a *Call of Duty* fan."

"Me too! The original. It may be an older game, but I still like it best. I'm focusing on *Operation: Absolute Zero* now. I'd rather play the old one, but I play online and all those guys want to play the newer versions, so I've had to do that. But when I play by myself, I always go back to the original."

"You play online?" He nodded. "My brother's online name is DozerBrother."

His eyes lit up. "No way! I play with him! He's on my team!"

"No kidding? That's cool! So you guys play, what, every Thursday night at nine?"

"Yeah. Been doing that for a couple of years now." Jerrica breathed a sigh of relief. She'd finally found something he was interested in!

"He won't miss it. If he does, he's foul for a whole week until the next time. And his wife is pretty happy about it too. Instead of playing every second of every day, he's gone to playing on Thursday night with you guys and only playing by himself a couple of times a week."

He shook his head. "I don't have time to play all the time either. Between work and work and more work, I really don't have a lot of extra time," he said with a laugh.

"I hear you. I don't have a lot of extra time either. Seems like every time I have something planned, I get called in because they're shorthanded and I miss out."

"What do you do?" he asked, and she felt like she'd won the lottery. He was finally engaged in the conversation.

"I'm an ER nurse over at County General."

"Oh! Cool! That's a great profession, but I know what you mean. There's a shortage of nurses, so I bet you get plenty of overtime."

"I do, more than I'd like. I was ten minutes late leaving tonight. I'm supposed to get my charting done during my shift, but it just wasn't possible. There were too many patients who needed attention."

"I hear ya." Watching his fingers slide down the sides of the beer bottle made her heart skip a beat, and she wished they were touching her instead. "So, tell me—what was the most interesting case you've seen come through the ER?"

"Hmmm. Let's see … I'd have to say it was the guy who came in impaled on a tobacco stake."

"Oh my god! Did he survive?"

She laughed. "Yeah! Took us forever to get all the splinters out of his skin. I think there are some still embedded in him. Had to have emergency surgery. First time I've seen wood shavings in an operating suite!"

"Were you in on that?"

"No, but I was off shift, so I went up to the observation area to watch. It was a tricky surgery, but he was lucky. It didn't hit any major organs and he's fine now. But when he came in, we were sure he was a goner."

"Wow. That was some skill on the surgeon's part, huh?"

"Yep. It was Dr. Milay. He's really good at what he does."

"Sounds like it." That sexy voice trailed off and he sat silent again.

Go for broke, Jerrica, she told herself. "You know, I could sit and listen to you talk all day long."

His brow dipped low and his cheekbones came up in a grimace. "What? Why?"

Take a chance. "Because you've got the sexiest voice I've ever heard."

"Me?"

"Yeah, you."

"If that's a pickup line—"

"It's not."

"Well, that's a shame, because if it were, it would be working," he said and took another swallow of beer.

Jerrica laughed. "Seriously?"

"Yeah. Seriously. That's the first time anybody's said the word 'sexy' in reference to me."

Now it was Jerrica's turn to be shocked. "You're joking, right?" He shook his head. "Well, I don't know who you've been hanging out with, but they obviously need the services of a good ophthalmologist because they must be totally blind."

He finally turned his head and looked straight into her eyes. "You know, I like you better when you're not drunk."

"You know, I like me better when I'm not drunk too!" she said and laughed again, and that time, he joined her. "But, you know, if nothing else came of it, at least I got to meet you."

He turned to look at his beer bottle again and Jerrica was pretty sure the conversation was over. But he surprised her. "And I got to meet you. Would you let me take you to dinner?"

"Absolutely. I'd like that. Where and when?"

He shrugged. "How about Joey's Seafood and Tuesday night?"

"Sounds great," she said with a grin. "Maybe seven?"

"Seven is good. I'll pick you up."

"I should give you my … Wait. You already know where I live," she said, her face burning.

"Yep. I do." Glancing around the bar, he set his bottle down on the tabletop. "I should probably get out of here. It was a rough day."

"Yeah, we heard the transmissions from the fire department."

He nodded. "Yeah. We've had a string of fires lately, and I'd call some of them suspicious. So we have to be on our toes."

"I should probably go too. I'm exhausted."

"From the kid with the heroin overdose?"

She nodded. "That was horrible."

He stood. "That's gotta be hard."

"It is. Every time. Especially people so young." She stood too. Jerrica sighed inwardly. She'd finally gotten him to talk, and now they had to go. But they were going out on Tuesday night! That was something to look forward to.

"Come on. I'll walk you to your car." Landon handed a twenty to Lucky and walked a couple of paces behind her as they left. She hadn't noticed before, but it appeared all his buddies and her friends had split, probably to go hook up. Thank god they weren't going to be there to cat-call and whistle as she and Landon walked out.

A little giggle broke from her lips when he walked right up to her little car. "Aaaaaand you know my car."

He laughed. "Yeah! Drives pretty good too."

"How'd you get home?"

"Walked to the convenience store down the street from you and had a cab pick me up."

Rolling her eyes, she sighed loudly. "I'm so sorry. I should pay for that."

"Nope. My decision. Like I said, I'm just glad I was there." The locks popped up when she hit the button on her key fob, and he opened her door. "Here you go. Drive safely. And text me when you get there and get locked in so I know you're safe."

Oh my god! Yes! she heard her inner teenager scream. "I will, and thanks."

"You're welcome. Take care and I'll see you Tuesday at seven."

"Yep. I'll be waiting."

"Goodnight, Jerrica."

"Night, Landon." The little car started right up, and as she pulled away, she looked back to see him give her a little wave. She tooted the tinny horn on the car in reply and drove down the darkened street toward her duplex.

"Goodnight, Jerrica." If she could have one wish, it would be that she could hear him say that in his bed and in his arms.

* * *

They were busy, a lot busier than they'd been in weeks. It was a full moon, and when those came around, the emergency room was usually swamped. That night was no exception. There were at least five accidents, including a guy thrown from a horse and somebody with a hatchet in their head. She'd been busy with the cowboy, so she hadn't taken the hatchet. Based on what she'd heard, it was a true blessing that she'd missed it.

But about eleven o'clock, her world turned upside down when she heard the transmission over the radio at the ER desk: "Structure fire, Stations Two and Three; structure fire, Stations Two and Three. Four twenty-two East First Street. Repeat, structure fire, Stations Two and Three, four twenty-two East First Street."

"Copy that, dispatch. Station Two responding. ETA, four minutes."

"Copy that, dispatch. Station Three responding. ETA, six minutes."

Jerrica spun toward the desk. "Did they say Station Two?"

The health unit coordinator at the desk nodded. "Yep."

Oh, god. Isn't that Landon's station? She tried hard to remember. Mina walked past and Jerrica grabbed her. "Aren't Landon and his buddies at Station Two?"

Mina gave her an odd look, her brow wrinkled. "Yeah. Why?"

"They just got called out."

"Happens all the time," her friend said and sashayed away toward a dog bite victim.

She doesn't seem the least bit concerned, Jerrica groused to herself, and then she realized Mina, Brandy, and the rest of her friends thought of the guys as entertainment. Landon wasn't entertainment to her. He was a person, a smart, handsome, kind person. It was hard to work and listen at the same time, and her patients couldn't afford for her to be distracted, but she had to know. There was a lot of chatter, and then it got quiet. They'd gone to another channel to work. Made sense.

"Now keep that clean and dry and go to your family physician in two weeks to have it looked at. He can most likely take the stitches out himself," Dr. Blankenship told her patient. "Wait right here and I'll get your discharge papers ready. You can go ahead and get dressed."

"Okay. Thanks." They left the cubicle as the guy started to pull his clothes on.

"He's got to stay here," the doctor whispered to Jerrica.

"Yeah. GSW. Police on their way?" she whispered back, and the doctor nodded. "Okay. I'll keep him here." Any gunshot wounds had to be reported to the police department, even though the guy had accidentally shot himself in the leg. Thank goodness it was just a flesh wound.

She parked herself outside the cubicle to wait for the officers she knew were coming. In less than two minutes, she looked up and saw Barry Hudson hustling through the doors. "You come for my GSW?" she asked and tipped her head toward the cubicle.

To her surprise, Barry was out of breath and appeared to be in quite a hurry. "Yeah. Did I understand correctly? Accidentally shot himself in the leg?"

She nodded. "Yep."

"Any indication he's lying?"

"Nope."

"I'll talk to him, but I've gotta get going." Being so brusque was unusual for Barry. He usually hung around and chatted to keep from being called out again.

"You okay?"

"No. This fire downtown ... It's pretty bad. I need to get back down there. We're trying to clear a five-block radius and keep everybody out."

Her heart trembled in her chest. "That bad?"

"Yeah. It's the old Michaels' Mercantile building. That thing is full of junk and takes up half a city block. It's probably going to take down everything in the block with it."

"Oh, wow. I heard them call in Stations Two and Three," Jerrica offered, hoping he'd cough up more information.

"They're calling in all the rest except Station One. They're on standby for any other fires or problems but otherwise, everybody will be down there. It's a mess. They're talking about calling in the volunteer departments from all over the area." With that pronouncement, he disappeared into the cubicle. Jerrica wanted to hear what he was saying to her patient, but she was numb with fear and concentrating was difficult.

The next two people through the door were a young man and his girlfriend, and she had a fork stuck through her cheek from the inside out. "What happened?" Jerrica asked as she did the intake work.

"I tah ah ah sha," she mumbled.

"She tripped on a shoe. She was eating as she walked across the room, and she tripped, and when she stood up, she looked like this," the young man said, his face pale and upper lip sweating.

"You need to go into the restroom, wet a paper towel, put it on your forehead, and lie down on the floor with your feet resting up the wall. Now," Jerrica ordered. "She's going to be fine." The man disappeared through the cubicle doorway and she smiled at the young woman. "You're going to be okay. It looks a lot worse than it is, really. I promise."

As soon as the paperwork was filled out, she dumped it into the system, went to the restroom to check on the boyfriend, and headed back to the desk. She was about to pick up her tablet and pull up her next patient when the radio crackled to life. "Community General, this is central dispatch. Four injuries en route via ambulance. ETA of first is three minutes."

"Roger that, central. Any idea what's coming?" Mallory, the HUC, asked.

"Negative. Variety. Floor collapse in the call downtown."

"Roger. We're standing by."

Before Mallory had a chance to say anything, Jerrica yelled out, "Clearing cubicles five through eight!" as she ran down the hallway. In a few minutes, she was joined by two more nurses, and together they readied all four cubicles for burn injuries.

By the time they ran back out into the hallway, the automatic doors at the ambulance bay were sliding open and buses were lining up. Elevator doors were opening and doctors were heading in from all over the hospital. Jerrica and another nurse directed them to the four cubicles and waited.

An EMT pushed a gurney with an IV bag hanging. "Male. Approximately thirty-five years old. Head injury and burns."

"Cubicle five," Jerrica directed and watched as they wheeled the man past her.

The second came through the door with a gurney. "Male. Approximately twenty-eight years old. Crushing injury to lower extremities, and burns."

"Cubicle six," another nurse barked.

"Male. Approximately thirty-two years old. Closed head injury, burns," the third EMT called out.

Mina had stepped into the fray. "Cubicle seven."

When the fourth gurney rolled in, there was quite a commotion in that general direction, and Jerrica heard someone shout, "I'm not hurt! Just let me go back!"

"Sir, please, cooperate with us," she heard the EMT request. "You have a head lac and you were unconscious for—"

"I'm fine! Please! I need to get back." The voice sounded familiar, and Jerrica's heart almost thudded to a stop.

Landon.

"Cubicle eight," she told the EMT and pointed.

"Jerrica! Thank god! Somebody who'll listen to me!" she heard Landon yelling back at her as they rolled the gurney into the cubicle. "Let me out of here! I've got to—"

"HEY!" she barked into his face as soon as she was in the cubicle. "You need to calm down! Just let us look at you, okay?"

"Please, just let me out of here. We need everybody down there. I need to go back. Jerrica, please, just—"

"Absolutely not. Not until we've checked you out."

"But I need to—"

She interrupted him by turning to the EMT. "Did you say he had a period of unconsciousness?"

"Yes, ma'am," the man said and nodded.

"Yeah, well, you need to go back down there, pass out in a burning building, and never come out," she announced and slapped Landon's shin. "You sit right there. Don't you go anywhere. I've got to see to that wound. Any burns?"

"No. I'm not burned." The EMT had already wandered out of the cubicle, and Landon was finally settling down a bit.

Reaching up to the top of his head, she parted his hair and took a good look. "Good. Let's look at that laceration you've got on … Oh, yeah. You need stitches for that." She set about getting out antiseptic wash and a suture kit. "I'm probably going to have to shave a little bit to either side of the stitch line. And as deep as it is, I can tell you right now the doctor's going to want an X-ray to check you for a concussion."

Landon had gone from ordering to pleading. "Please, Jerrica? Please let me go? I swear, I'll be careful, but I need to—"

She glared down into his face. "Sit right there. You need to sit. Right. There. I mean it. You're going nowhere, do you understand?"

He rolled his eyes like a fourteen-year-old. "Yeah, yeah. I get it. Just hurry up, okay?"

"I don't tell you how to do your job, and you're not going to tell me how to do mine. We clear on that?" she snapped and glared at him again.

His eyebrows shot up and he grinned. "Yes, ma'am!"

"Good. No more of that shit. Let me get one of the doctors in here to give me the go-ahead for suturing and we'll see what he says."

"Did somebody say doctor?" Dr. Reed asked with a chuckle.

Jerrica nodded. "Yes, sir. Subcue head lac approximately six centimeters in length with exposure of epicranial aponeurosis."

"In layman's terms," Dr. Reed explained as he smiled at Landon, "you've cracked your head open, firefighter. We've got two options here, and one won't require shaving around the laceration."

Landon brightened. "Yeah?"

"It'll have to be shaved if it's sutured, but we won't

have to shave it if we use staples." Landon grimaced and winced at the same time. "I know, sounds barbaric, but it works."

"Then staples it is," the firefighter said.

"I'll have to do those. But first, if we're going to put staples in it, you're going down for an X-ray."

"I don't need an—"

"You *do* need an X-ray. You could have a concussion. I'll call radiology and tell them you're on your way," Dr. Reed said. As he walked out the door, he turned back and looked straight at Landon. "Don't give her any trouble."

The man sitting on the gurney sighed loudly. "Yes, sir."

"Let's roll you," Jerrica said and released the brake on the gurney.

Landon shook his head. "I can walk."

"No. You absolutely cannot walk. We're responsible for you while you're here," she announced.

But he struggled to get up. "No, I can … Ohhhhhh," he moaned and lay back down.

"Uh-huh. Stay right there." Jerrica pushed the gurney toward the doorway.

When they cleared it, Dr. Reed was standing right outside, looking at another chart on his tablet. He glanced up as they passed. "Behave. Don't make me call your dad or your brother."

"No. Please, god, don't do that," Landon muttered.

Jerrica was confused. Why would Dr. Reed say that

to Landon? "Your dad or your brother?" she asked as she pushed him along.

"Yeah."

She waited.

"I'm sure you know my brother, Brandon."

Jerrica kept pushing him and then stopped dead in the middle of the hallway. "Brandon Fox? *Doctor* Brandon Fox?" *Oh my god, THAT'S why he looks so familiar!* her brain shrieked. "That means—"

He sighed again. "Yes. Dr. Robert Fox is my dad. My mother was his nurse for years. I'm the disappointment of the family," he announced.

"I, I, I didn't make the connection. You and Brandon—"

"Yep. Twins. I'm the older by like twelve minutes. So congratulations to me, huh?"

"Oh my god. Why aren't you a doctor too?" she asked without even thinking about it.

"Because I didn't *want* to be a doctor. I wanted to be a firefighter. Always. Ever since I was a little bitty boy. It's all I ever wanted to do. Of course, I've been told consistently that I'm an idiot, so there's that." There was something in his voice, an edge, that told her his decision had been a sore spot in his family his whole life.

"I-I-I-I'm sorry. I mean, there's nothing wrong with being a firefighter. Is your sister—"

"Medical? No. She was supposed to be. Second year of undergrad when she … when the incident happened.

She didn't finish. She's actually a barista at a coffee shop, and she struggles to hold that job."

"Oh, god, I'm so sorry. I just, I mean, I don't know what to say."

"There's nothing *to* say. It is what it is." As soon as the words left his mouth, he went silent.

Dear god, I opened a swarming hornet's nest with all that, Jerrica thought. She felt terrible. Landon had been demeaned all his life about his career choice, and his sister was so crippled by her attack that she could barely function. Life wasn't fair—at all. "You know, I admire you for going through with your choice even though it sounds like you had nobody to support you."

"I have to admit, it hasn't been easy. I see my family. I mean, I have relationships with them, but we just don't talk about work when we're together. Period. If we do, my dad gets huffy, my mother gets weepy, my brother gets belligerent, and my sister withdraws even more. I mean, all my mother has ever said that could pass as support is, 'Now, if you're at a fire, call us so we know you're still alive.'"

That made sense to Jerrica. "Do you want to call them now?"

A low rumble of a chuckle rolled from his throat. "No. I'll let them sweat for a little while."

She couldn't help but snicker. "You're evil, know that?"

"Yeah. I'm evil. I'm the devil incarnate. Satan's favorite minion here."

"You know, honestly, I like this side of you better than the one that doesn't talk and doesn't want to be part of the things going on around him." She rolled the gurney into an x-ray room. "Now, let's get you on this table and the tech will be here in just a minute."

"I'm here, I'm here. What've we got?" an x-ray tech named Theo asked as he skimmed over the order.

"Scalp lac and possible concussion. Dr. Reed wants a film."

"Got it. Step out into the hallway, please," the young man told Jerrica. As soon as she closed the door, she could hear him talking to Landon. A few minutes passed and the door opened. "You can take him back. We'll have the results down there by the time you get back to his ER hole."

"Thanks. Okay. Climb on, firefighter. I'll take you for another little ride," Jerrica said with a smile, and she noticed Landon wasn't as cocky as before. "You okay?"

"My head's really hurting now. I think it's from all this moving around." She watched as he climbed back onto the gurney and once he was still, she threw the side rail up and away they went.

By the time she got him back into his cubicle, Dr. Reed was walking in. "Okay, young man, it seems you've got a mild concussion. Very mild. But nothing to take lightly. So you'll need someone who'll wake you every two hours throughout the night to make sure you're okay."

Landon shrugged. "I don't have anybody. I live alone."

"I suppose I could call your dad and—"

"NO! Don't call my dad! Please! Isn't there something else we could do?"

"You can stay here."

"No. I don't want to stay here. I want to go home."

"Either you get somebody to stay with you or you stay here. I can't release you if I don't know that you'll have someone with you."

"But I—"

"No. Either here or with someone."

Landon rolled his eyes. "I really don't want to—"

"He can stay with me." Both men turned to stare at Jerrica. "I have a guest bedroom, and I'd know what to do if something went wrong in the night. He can come home with me." She stared straight into Landon's face. "You can come home with me. You're welcome to."

"Um, I dunno about—"

"It's that or stay here, firefighter. What'll it be?" Dr. Reed asked.

The look he gave her was all puppy-dog eyes. "You're sure it would be okay?"

"Of course. No problem at all. I can take you by your place to get some clean clothes, even shower, and then I can drive you to my place. We'll go get your truck later."

"But you'll be dead on your feet tomorrow when you have to come to work," Landon pointed out.

Dr. Reed tapped his tablet. "Nope. Jerrica, I can give you tomorrow off. I'll sign off on it as an external assignment and they'll let you have the day. After about ten o'clock tomorrow morning, if he's okay, he can go home. And you can get some sleep. How does that sound?"

"See?" Jerrica said, folding her arms across her chest. "It's all worked out. Are you coming home with me, or do you want to stay here?"

"Hope that bed's a queen or my feet will hang off the end," he said and laughed.

"Yes. It's a queen. You'll be fine. Anytime you want to release him, Dr. Reed, I'll take him on."

Dr. Reed picked up his stapler and went to work. "No problem. Let's get these staples in and then I'll get the coordinator to bring his release paperwork. As soon as he's released, you're free to take him." Jerrica watched as Landon sat perfectly still, but he winced with every *click* of the tool. "And you, young man," the doctor said and pointed right into Landon's face. "You do what she tells you to, you hear me? I'd better not find out you gave her trouble."

Landon held his hands up in mock surrender. "No, sir. I wouldn't do that. She's being exceptionally nice to me. It wouldn't do for me to be rude to her with her extending hospitality to me."

Surveying his work, the doctor smiled. "Good. Go. Get some rest. And check in with your regular doctor sometime in the next two days. Take care." With that, the physician was gone.

"Guess you're my captive for the evening, huh?" Jerrica asked and laughed.

"Looks like it. Hey, could you check on Big Dog? I mean Carlos. He's one of the other guys brought in. He was with me when the collapse took place, and I want to know he's okay."

"Okay. Hang on and stay right here." Jerrica left the cubicle and made her way to the central desk, straight up to the HUC. "Need to know about a firefighter named Carlos who was brought in by bus."

The HUC looked up at her. "Carlos Moreno?"

"I guess so. Carlos is all I know."

"Let me see … Oh. Um, I'm sorry. They did all they could for him, but his injuries were too severe."

Jerrica's eyes almost bugged out of her head and her jaw dropped. "You're kidding."

"Nope. Severe closed head injury and burns. But the closed head injury was what killed him. Looks like your patient in there was very lucky. They were together when they were pulled out."

The dazed sensation hadn't faded when she stepped into Landon's space. "Carlos Moreno?"

"Yeah."

"He didn't make it."

A look passed over Landon's face, one Jerrica didn't recognize. He was breathless when he wheezed out, "Oh, god. We were right there together. Five feet from each other. How could he be … Why am I not … Oh, god. He's got a wife and two kids. Are you sure?"

She nodded. "Yes. The HUC just read me the records. I'm sorry, Landon. I'm sure you guys were close."

"Yes. We were. I can't believe it. I just … I can't believe it." Bewildered. That was the best way she could describe the look on his face. And horrified—horrified that it could've been him and it wasn't. Maybe he thought it should've been him instead of a man with a wife and children.

But it hadn't been. Landon was right there, and he'd be fine. What surprised her most was how glad she was that it hadn't been him. Just the idea that she wouldn't see him again … She couldn't even think about that. "Look, I think you've had enough for one day. I'm going to clock out and I'll come back and get you so I can take you to get some clothes and then to my apartment. Okay? Will you stay right here?"

"Yeah." His voice had a hollow sound to it and Jerrica was a little worried about him. She hadn't even cleared the doorway when she heard a voice call his name from out in the hallway, and she knew without looking who it was.

"Landon? What the hell? Why didn't you call one of us? We heard about this on the news, for god's sake!" Dr. Brandon Fox stood there in the doorway of the cubicle, shouting into the space. "I can't believe you'd put us through that!"

"You don't work at this hospital. What are you doing here?" Landon asked, and Jerrica was shocked at his tone.

"I came to check on you, but I can see you're fine. I heard one of your coworkers isn't so fine."

"You're right. He's not. And he was less than five feet from me, so I'd appreciate it if you'd stay at least that far away. This hasn't been my best day."

"You're right. This hasn't been your best day. That could've been you, Landon. *This* is why you're an idiot! *This* is why Mom and Dad stay so upset with you! *This* is why everybody thinks you're crazy to do a job that could kill you for less than my receptionist makes every year! Are you about ready to do something that actually makes some *sense* for a change?"

In a split second, she saw a side of Landon Fox that she hadn't seen before. The usually mild-mannered, mostly quiet guy who had trouble carrying on a conversation suddenly came to life. "Something that makes some *sense*? You know what, I hope your fucking house never catches on fire, because a bunch of guys doing something that doesn't make any sense will show up and try to save it for you! And god forbid one of them should get hurt doing it. You won't tell them thank you—you'll tell them how *stupid* they are! Do you have *no respect* for people who aren't just like you?"

"You're exasperating," Brandon said and threw up his hands. "Nobody can talk any sense into you."

"And nobody seems to be able to get through to you

what a pompous ass you are! Go home, Brandon. Go home to your *wife*. Go home and tell her all about your dumb sumbitch brother who doesn't have any more sense than to run into burning buildings to try to save people's lives. Tell her *that*." Landon spun toward Jerrica, his eyes glowing with anger. "Can you get me the hell out of here and away from him? Now?"

"Yes. Here—sign this." She handed him the one paper that was mandatory for him to sign before he could leave, along with a pen. In seconds, he'd signed it and handed it back. "We'll drop it at the desk. Come on. I don't have time to find you a wheelchair. Besides, you can walk out of here."

"Thank you." She waited as he stood at the side of the bed, wobbled just a little, and then steadied himself. As he stepped toward her in the hallway, he turned back to Brandon. "Either support me or stay the hell away from me." Not even looking at Jerrica, he strode down the hallway, then turned and glared at his brother who still stood in the cubicle's doorway. "Oh, and by the way, I made lieutenant. Lieutenant, Brandon. Tell Mom and Dad *that*. You're all invited to my promotion ceremony, not that I'd expect you to come. Matter of fact, I'd be shocked if you did. Celebrating *any* kind of success I have would just be too much for you, now wouldn't it?" He spun again and strode right through the automatic doors, Jerrica right on his heels.

She dropped into the driver's seat and waited, but

he said nothing. After waiting as long as she could, she asked, "Where am I going?"

He rubbed his eyes and sighed. "Just drive. I'll tell you where to turn."

The little G6 rolled down the darkened city streets. In the distance, there was a faint glow, and Jerrica knew he could see it too—what remained of the active fire. She'd halfway thought he'd ask her to drive by there, but he hadn't, and she was glad. He didn't need to see that. He just needed some rest.

And somebody who believed in him.

CHAPTER 3

Landon sat there as Jerrica drove, and he fought back tears. He and Big Dog had been friends. Not the kind of friendships he had with Stingray, Rodeo, and Juice, because they were all single like he was. Big Dog had a family. Megan was pretty, and the kids, Paige and Edward, were cute and smart. They'd invited him for dinner a few times, and he'd enjoyed playing video games with Edward and looking at Big Dog's restored fifty-seven Chevy. They were nice people.

That woman and those kids would wake up tomorrow morning with their whole world falling down around them. Their husband and father was a hero, but that wouldn't tuck them in at night, or buy their school lunches, or pay the insurance on the house or car. He hoped she had some decent life insurance on him, because the department didn't offer much. "Turn left at the next corner and it's the third house on the right." He waited as she turned the corner and drove toward his house. "That one right there."

As soon as she was parked, he got out, but she did too. "You don't have to come in. I can—"

"Oh, yes. I do have to come in. I don't want you going in by yourself. You could black out and hit your head or something."

"It's a pig sty."

"I bet it's not."

He shuffled to the door as the weariness of the day hit him. God, how would he ever manage to get anything together and get back to the car? Once the door was unlocked, he hit the light switch and held the door open for her, then headed for the bedroom.

"What did you say?" he called out as he pulled some things from his dresser.

"I said this is very nice. And it's sure not a pig sty. Nice artwork."

"Thanks. Got that from here and there when I went on trips."

"I like it."

He got his toothpaste and toothbrush, a razor and shaving cream, and his hairbrush, and threw it all in the bag with his clothes. As he stepped into the living room, he asked, "What time can I come home tomorrow?"

"About ten tomorrow morning, but you'll have to check in with me at least twice later in the day."

He nodded. "Okay. You'll take me to get my car?"

"Sure. Not a problem."

"Okay. I think I've got everything."

They hadn't gotten two blocks through the subdivision when Jerrica said, "Landon, I'm sorry your brother said those things to you."

"Don't apologize for him. That's on him. He's an ass."

"I wanted so badly to say something, but he's a doctor, and I'm a nurse, and—"

"No apology necessary. Not your fault."

"I just think it's so unfair that he said those things. From where I sit, you're a hero."

"I'm no hero. I'm still alive and Big Dog is dead."

"Landon?" He knew what she was going to say and he didn't want to face her. "Landon, look at me." When he finally turned to her, she said, "That's the luck of the draw. It could've been you, but it wasn't. Next time, it may be. But for today, and tomorrow, you're still here. That's all you've got."

Holy shit, that's deep, he thought as she drove on. *And she's right too.* The next time it could very easily be him. They pulled up in front of her apartment and she threw the little car into park. Without looking at her, Landon said softly, "Thanks for bringing me here. I didn't want to stay in that hospital another minute."

"You're welcome. Now come on in and let's get you settled."

He remembered a little about her apartment, but he hadn't seen the guest room before. It was tidy and tastefully decorated, even though it was a little on the feminine side, but he would've been surprised if it hadn't been. After showering and carrying out his bedtime routine in the hall bathroom, he headed back to the bedroom, changed into his flannel lounge pants and a tee, and crawled under the covers. That was when he noticed it. *Damn, this mattress is comfortable!* The sheets were super soft, and the comforter was light but warm. He was about to turn off the lamp when there was a rap on the door. "Come in."

"Hey. Just wanted you to know that I'll be in here every two hours, remember? So don't be surprised. I'm just going to wake you enough to get you to talk to me a little, but you may not remember in the morning if you're sleeping soundly. Is there anything I can get you before we turn out the lights?"

"Nah. I'm fine. And by the way, this bed is amazing. Thanks so much, Jerrica. Really. I appreciate it."

"You're welcome. See you in a couple of hours. Night, Landon."

"Goodnight, Jerrica." He waited until the door clicked shut before he turned out the light, then lay there in the darkness, listening to her move around until there was nothing but silence. As he drifted away, he could hear Carlos's voice and see his face, laughing and animated in the memory of the last time Landon had been to their home for dinner. It was beyond sad, but there wasn't a thing he could do about it except try to do better the next time.

And there would be a next time. Of that he was certain.

* * *

The sun was peeking in around the curtains when Landon woke. It took him a second or two to remember where he was, but when he did, he smiled. He was in Jerrica's apartment.

Thinking about her made him smile. Talking to her made him smile. Hell, everything about the petite, blond nurse made him giddy. He loved the lilt in her voice, the sparkle of those blue eyes, and that body that called to him. Jerrica was the embodiment of everything he'd ever dreamed of. Someone who was kind. Someone who was smart. Someone who was funny. And someone who could handle him. He'd been damn near out of control the night before when they brought him in, but when he'd started in on her she'd snapped right back at him. She wouldn't take any shit off him.

But he could also see that she wouldn't give him shit. That was good, because that was all he'd ever gotten from women before—shit, and a lot of it. Especially Shonda. That bitch … He'd never wished a soul dead, but if the earth opened up and swallowed her, it wouldn't hurt his feelings one bit. Just thinking about her made his head pound. He wasn't sure who he disliked more, her or his brother, but he really didn't have any use for either of them.

His phone screen said it wasn't even nine o'clock yet, so he decided to roll over and go back to sleep. When he woke again, it was almost ten and the air around him was filled with the aroma of fresh coffee. That made him sit up and take notice, and he swung his legs off the side of the bed and sat there in his lounge pants and tee, scratching his head. He let out a little yelp when he hit the staples he'd forgotten were in his scalp.

"You okay in there?" her voice called out.

"Yeah. Forgot about my staples."

"Keep your hands off them," she barked.

"Yes, ma'am." That made him smile too.

"Coffee's ready. Bacon and eggs are a few minutes out. Biscuits and gravy too."

Hot damn, and she can cook! Fishing around, he found the hairbrush he'd brought with him and worked at making some sense out of his thick, dark hair without hitting his incision. It was harder than he'd ever imagined. When he decided he was at least presentable, he slipped on his slippers, opened the door, and peered out.

He could see Jerrica from the hallway as she moved about in the kitchen, a skillet and spatula in her hands. He'd never thought of a woman moving about the kitchen as something that could be graceful—god knew his mother had always looked like she was angry that she had to attempt to make something edible—but Jerrica actually looked at home that way, the sash of her bibbed apron tied in a neat bow at the small of her back. Jesus, she was amazing! Landon was growing a little concerned about their date. If she had any feminine wiles he hadn't seen yet, he was doomed. What he'd already experienced was more than enough to do him in.

"There you are! Have a seat. How do you take your coffee?"

"Black. I'll get it."

"No. You're my guest. I'll get it for you. You just sit. Feel okay?"

He gave her a nod. "Yes, ma'am. I'm okay. Little bit of a headache, but that's about it. Although I have to say, it's almost impossible to brush my hair this way."

"I know. It'll be impossible to wash it too, but I'll do that for you before I take you to your car. I know how without fouling your incision, and it'll feel better to have all the blood and antiseptic stuff out of it."

"Yes it will. It's miserable right now. Itches something horrible," he added.

"I can take care of that too. It'll be fine." A cup of steaming coffee appeared in front of him, followed by a plate with two beautiful over-medium eggs and three pieces of crispy bacon. "Oh, and here," she said, setting a plateful of golden toast in front of him.

"You didn't have to go to all this trouble," he announced as he picked up his cup of coffee.

"I've gotta eat too. Thought I might as well make you some. Just made sense!" she said with a laugh.

He couldn't help but chuckle. "Yeah. Guess so. You gonna sit with me and eat?"

"Sure am." In seconds, she was right there. There was a mischievous glint in her eye when she said, "Never thought we'd be eating breakfast together before our first date."

Landon let out a laugh. "Me either!"

They laughed and talked and the time flew. Landon could honestly say he hadn't felt that comfortable with a woman in years. At ten forty-five Jerrica asked, "Are you about ready to go get your car?"

He wished she hadn't said that. Instead, he wanted to stay there and talk to her all day, but he couldn't and he knew it. "Sure. So how do I get this shampoo job?"

"We'll go in the bathroom and you can kneel beside the tub. I can do it that way. Come on."

Thirty minutes later, his hair was washed and dried, and she'd put something on the incision that made it stop itching immediately. "Dr. Reed would probably be angry with me for this, but it won't hurt anything and you'll get some relief. Now you can shower with the hand-held sprayer and get ready to go." With that, she disappeared from the bathroom and left him standing there.

But he'd caught it—that little hitch in her breath when he'd whipped his tee off over his head and stood there in front of her bare-chested. She'd apparently liked what she saw, and that made him happy. He wanted her to see more of him—a lot more.

Showered and dressed, Landon picked up everything he'd brought and put it all back in his bag before he made his way out into the living room. He could hear her singing in her own bathroom and he smiled at the sound. She was like a breath of fresh air. As he waited, he made his way back into the kitchen and began loading the dishwasher. She hadn't taken time to do it, so it was the least he could do in exchange for the wonderful breakfast she'd fed him.

"You didn't have to do that! I would've done it," Landon heard her say and turned.

Jerrica stood there in a yellow sundress with little golden thong sandals on those tiny little feet, and he knew he'd never seen anything more beautiful. Her long, golden tresses were caught up in a half tail with a sunflower hair clip, and she was wearing pearls. How classy could one woman be? "Look at you. You're amazing." The minute he said the words, he could feel his cheeks heating up.

"Awww, thank you. That's sweet." She fingered the beads. "They're not real, but I love them."

"They look real enough on you." *Shit, that sounded lame!* he thought as soon as the words came out.

"Thanks." There was an awkward pause in the conversation before she said, "Ready to go?"

"Sure. I think I got everything." He held the door for her as they left and she locked it behind them. "Looks different in the daylight," he said with a grin.

She didn't look at him when she said, "Yeah. First

time you've seen it in the daylight, huh?" He could hear the embarrassment in her voice.

"Yeah. Pretty neighborhood."

"Very quiet too. I enjoy living here."

"I can see why."

As soon as the car doors closed and she started the car, she asked, "Where's your truck?"

"At the station."

"Duh." Her cheeks pinked, and then she asked, "So what is that subdivision called? The one where you live?"

"Oh. Bailey Acres."

There was silence for a few seconds before she said, "You own the house."

"Yes."

"Those are nice houses."

"They are." Where was she going with that line of conversation? He couldn't imagine. "I'm surprised you haven't bought a house."

Her face clouded over and he sucked in a breath. After what seemed like forever, she said, "Student loans."

"Ah. Makes sense. Sorry."

"Yeah. Me too. But at least I can earn myself a living."

"I've had to pay for a few fire schools. Not cheap. I can't imagine a four-year degree."

"Your parents didn't pay for them?"

"No. But they paid for my brother's education. They

were paying for my sister's." Landon hoped he didn't sound too bitter.

"Oh. Because you weren't going to medical school."

"I see you're understanding what I'm not saying," he muttered as he looked out the window and watched the scenes of small town America go by.

"I'm sorry they've treated you that way. It's so unfair."

"Your parents didn't pay for your education?" he asked, not thinking about what he was saying.

"No. My dad's a truck driver and my mom works at the mall."

Well, that was pretty fucking insensitive of me, he scolded himself as they rode along. "I'm sorry. I had no idea what your parents do for a living."

"Well, now you do. Landon, I'm the first person in my family to go to college."

"But your brother ..."

"*DozerBrother,* remember? He works for an excavating firm. He didn't go to college. Not even trade school."

Landon was left with nothing to say. The woman had worked hard and gone into debt to give herself something her family couldn't afford to provide for her. He finally came out with, "I admire your determination."

"Thanks."

They drove a good distance more before she said, "You're being kinda quiet."

"I'm thinking about what I'll be walking into at the station."

Her brow furrowed and then her eyebrows shot up. "Oh. Because of Carlos. Landon, I'm so sorry. We should've talked about it last night after we got to my place. I'm not usually so insensitive, but I was worried about you."

"It's okay. I'm just grateful that you agreed to take care of me."

As the car glided up in front of the station house, she smiled. "My pleasure. We still on for tonight?"

"If you still want to."

"I definitely want to."

"And I definitely want to too. See you this evening, then. Thanks for the ride. Bye," he said as he got out. God, he wished he could lean over and kiss her! That would've been a little premature.

"You're welcome. See you then. Bye."

He closed the car door and walked away but when he reached the station's door, he turned to see her give him a little wave as she drove away. He watched as her car disappeared down the street and around the corner.

And he already missed her.

* * *

The evening couldn't come around fast enough, and Landon found himself daydreaming about it all afternoon. Would they have a good time? Would she like him? He hoped she already did.

Crisp, pale blue broadcloth shirt and a pair of chinos. Landon looked himself up and down in the mirror and thought he looked pretty good. He added a pair of lace-up oxfords—very nice. *Now for the finishing touches.* He slipped on the signet ring Brandon had given him three Christmases before and the Panerai watch his parents had given him for his thirty-fifth birthday. His belt buckle was the same brushed steel as the watch, and he thought he looked pretty damn good for a man in his late thirties. It was certain that Jerrica was quite a bit younger than him, so he'd have to be careful to keep up his appearance.

The drive to her house seemed to take forever. There'd never been a time when he was as excited about a date as he was about that one. Not only was he hoping he'd get to know her better, but he wanted something to help him forget about Carlos, even for just a little while. The funeral would be hard, with Carlos's wife and kids front and center. Landon had been chosen to be a pallbearer, and he was worried. His head still hurt a little. What if he got dizzy and stumbled? The guys had assured him it would be fine, and he hoped that was true. All he really wanted at that moment was to stop thinking about it for a couple of hours.

Her little car was sitting there in front of her duplex when he pulled up, and he smiled. It was cute and sporty, and it suited her very well, but it looked tiny compared to his truck, kind of like Jerrica standing beside him. That thought almost made him laugh aloud. She was so bouncy and petite that every time he saw her, he thought she was cuter than the time before. He didn't even get a chance to knock on the door before it opened and her smile filled his vision. "Hey! That was quick!"

"I was watching for you. Come on in. I'll just be a minute." God, she was wearing another one of those sweet little dresses, and he could feel himself stiffening a little behind his fly. *Behave yourself,* he told his small brain. The gauzy fabric overlay on the skirt swished as she walked and he couldn't stop staring at her ass. Boy, what he'd give to see it bare, up close and personal. *Shit, Landon! What the fuck is wrong with you?*

He knew the answer already. Jerrica tripped triggers in him, switches that hadn't been flipped in a long time. Sure, he met plenty of women, but most of them were like her friends—try on a firefighter for size and then toss him aside. Most of his buddies were fine with that, but not Landon. Nope. He wanted a relationship, a real deal relationship, not something superficial and temporary. That adorable little ass swaying across the room in front of him represented every bit of that and more to him, and he couldn't afford to screw it all up with some impulsive behavior that would turn her off. His brain was fishing around for something to say when he noticed pictures on the other side of the room. "Your folks?"

"Yeah," she answered as she disappeared into her bedroom, but she kept talking. "My mom and dad. That's my brother and his wife over on the right."

"DozerBrother. I've never met him. Have you told him you've met me?"

"No. I figured I'd let you do that. Besides, I don't know what your gaming name is."

"Oh. It's HoseJockey." She started to laugh loudly. "What?"

"Oh, just something my friends said about your buddies having big hoses and knowing how to use them!" she answered, still barking with laughter. Landon could feel his cheeks heating up, and they had to be flaming red when she stepped out of the room. "Oh, my god, am I embarrassing you?"

"Uh, no. Why would you think—"

"Stop it. I'm sorry. I shouldn't have said that. It was kinda crass. I apologize."

"No, honestly, it sounds like something they'd brag about," he explained.

He could tell she was genuinely perplexed when she asked, "Why aren't you like that?"

He shrugged. "Because I don't have to be. I don't feel like I have anything to prove to anybody. I don't know what's wrong with guys like them, but I'd say it's feelings of insecurity or inadequacy."

"Wow. You don't cut them any slack, do you?" she asked as she stepped up closer to him.

"I guess I just hold myself to a different standard, that's all."

"And what would that be?"

This is it, Landon thought, his head almost swimming. It was his chance. He reached out, pressed a hand on either side of her waist, and drew her up close to him. "I don't brag. If I'm with somebody, she's happy with me, and I'm happy with her, there's no reason for all that posturing and chest-pounding."

He was thrilled when her arms rose and she clasped her hands behind his neck. "Ah, the strong, silent type. No Neanderthals here, huh?"

"Nope. Just a guy and a girl trying to get to know each other. All posturing and chest-thumping does is get in the way of who we really are. I could do that shit for months, but when it all came down to it, if you don't like who I really am, we've got nothing to work with. And honestly, I'm no kid. I don't have time for all that pretend stuff. I'm just me. I hope you feel comfortable just being who you are with me."

"God, Landon, you've seen me so drunk I didn't know who I was. There's really nothing I can hide, now is there?" she said with a giggle and stepped a little closer.

"Not much, no!" He hoped she could tell by his grin how happy he was to be that close to her. God, he wanted to kiss her! Before he could decide if he should, she rose up on her toes and pressed her lips to his.

It was all the encouragement Landon needed, and he came back at her, pulling her in against him so tightly that he hoped she had trouble breathing. As soon as she was snug in his arms, he tipped his head sideways and ran his tongue across the seam of her lips. She didn't disappoint—she opened to him instantly, and in seconds their tongues were thrashing against each other in an erotic dance Landon never wanted to come to an end. But when he finally pulled back, he gazed down into her breathless face and smiled. "Wow."

"Yeah, wow. And now I really don't want to go to dinner," she whispered up to him.

"Oh, no. We're going to dinner. We are absolutely, positively going to dinner." He gave her lips a quick peck and grinned. "I'm feeding you. After that, we'll make a decision on where this is going from there."

"Okay. I'm game. If I can keep you interested through dinner, I figure we'll have more options," she said with a laugh as she headed toward the door, Landon right behind her.

"I don't think you'll have any trouble keeping me interested, darlin'. I'm way too interested as it is," he threw in.

"Yeah. I noticed." That made his cheeks fire up again. Jesus, what was with the blushing already? He *never* blushed! The girl had an effect on him few others ever had.

Dinner. They had to make it through dinner. Was he coming back there to rip her clothes off and fuck her like there was no tomorrow?

God, he hoped so!

* * *

Jerrica loved Landon's big truck. It sat up high and she could see everything going on around them. Riding with her dad in the cab of his semi had always been something she'd loved, and she wondered why she'd never bought a pickup. "This is a nice truck."

"Thanks! I bought it with a bonus I got."

"You get bonuses?"

"Yeah. Performance bonuses based on the hours we work and training we've received throughout the year. They're not much. I say I bought it with the bonus; I used the bonus as the down payment. I had an old truck I traded in too, so I got a good deal on this one."

"That's good." Jerrica fished for something else to say. "By the way, you look really nice."

"Oh! Thanks! Yeah, I clean up pretty good, I guess."

"No, you clean up really good. I'd like to …" *Jump your bones,* she wanted to say. "… see your house again sometime."

"Oh, you'll see my house, trust me. I have plans for you to see my house. The inside, I mean."

"Yeah. I was just inside the front door. I'd like to see the rest of it."

Without looking at her, he asked, "Like my bedroom?"

Jerrica giggled. "Yeah. Like your bedroom."

"I'm sure that can be arranged eventually."

"So you're one of those slow movers, huh?"

"Nope. I'm one of those deliberate movers. I don't like to go off on a tangent. I like to plot a course and follow it."

"Not very spontaneous," she said as an observation.

"Oh, it can be very spontaneous, as long as the spontaneity is something that gets me where I'm going."

"Where do you want to go? I mean, with this?" she asked, hoping he'd come right out and say it.

"Whoa, babe! Let's slow down just a little bit. I think we both know where we want this to go in the near future, but I'm talking about the long haul here. I'm not a jump-in-bed kinda guy." Jerrica blushed. "Don't be embarrassed. It's fucking flattering as hell, but I don't want us to make some big mistake we're both going to regret. We're both old enough to know there's more to this than simple physical chemistry, although I have to say, ours is off the charts."

"Yeah. Seems that way." She was still a little embarrassed. Being that forward with a man wasn't something she did often. Matter of fact, never. And discussing a relationship outright? She'd *never* done that before! But something about Landon made her comfortable enough with him to say what she was thinking, and what she was thinking in that moment was about what kind of equipment he was packing in those superbly-fitted slacks. *Lawd, the man is fine!* she heard her brain whine long and low. “So how will we know?”

“Oh, we’ll know, trust me. But there’s something I forgot to ask you.” She waited as he pulled into a parking space at the restaurant, then turned to her. “How old are you?”

“Why?”

“Just answer the question, please.” His face was expressionless, and Jerrica couldn’t tell if she was about to dash everything she’d thought she’d been building with him.

“Um, I’m thirty-one.” When he didn’t answer, she asked, “How old are you?”

“Thirty-eight.”

“Landon, that’s only seven years.”

She could almost see him releasing the breath he’d been holding. “Yeah. I know. I’m sorry. My heart almost stopped beating. I was terrified you were going to tell me you were like twenty-five or something.”

Jerrica began to laugh hysterically. “Twenty-five? Oh my god, thank you! I haven’t been twenty-five in six years, and that makes me feel so damn good!”

Landon laughed along with her. “Good! I didn’t

want to offend you somehow, but seriously, I was afraid we were too far apart!"

"Nah. Now, if I was seventeen and you were twenty-four—"

"If you were seventeen, I wouldn't be messing with you. What do you think I am?" he asked, feigning horror.

"I think you're a really nice guy who wouldn't do that. Poor example," she said, still laughing. "Okay, if I were twenty-one and you were twenty-eight—"

"Yeah, that might be problematic. But we're both career people, and I can tell you've got your head on straight."

"And you've obviously got yours on straight. So I think we're in the clear there, don't you?"

Instead of answering her, he reached across the truck and took her hand. When his fingers tightened around it, she felt safe and cared for, even though he hadn't said a word. She just waited, and just when she was sure he wasn't going to say anything, he smiled. "I like you, Jerrica. I like you a lot, more than anybody else I've met in a long time. Maybe ever. I don't want this to go sideways on us because we get in too much of a hurry. I'm not going anywhere, and I don't think you are either, are you?"

"Nope. Not going anywhere unless you take me there," she answered with a grin.

"Good. Let's eat." He slipped out of the truck and she opened her door. As soon as he rounded the truck, he clucked at her. "Nuh-uh-uh. Not on my watch. You ride with me, I open your door and help you out and in. If that's too Neanderthal for you, then I don't know what to tell you."

"It's not too Neanderthal for me. I think it's sweet, and I love it." *I love you,* she almost said, then stopped herself. *Too soon!* her brain screamed, but she knew it was really too late. He was winning her heart, and she felt powerless to hold back. Landon was everything she'd ever wanted in a man, and he knew it. And that was fine by her.

The restaurant was beautiful. "I've never been here before," she whispered as the hostess seated them.

"They have the best shrimp in town, and sometimes they even have sea scallops," he said and picked up his menu.

"I love sea scallops!"

"Do you like crab?"

"Yeah. Love it."

He grinned. "We'll have to come back some Friday night. They have all-you-can-eat crab legs every Friday night."

"That sounds fantastic!" Jerrica looked over the menu and smiled. It was a beautiful place. There were nice linens on the tables, the silverware was correct for the place settings, and a candle in a beautiful crystal holder burned on the table. Everything was elegant without being stuffy. It made her feel like a princess in her own castle.

"I'll tell you what's fantastic." Landon peered at her over his menu. "Your face in this candlelight. You're beautiful, Jerrica. I hope you know that."

Tears sprang to her eyes. Her parents had tried, but she and her brother had been latchkey kids while their mom and dad worked. She'd been picked on at school because she was small, and everybody made fun of her because she didn't have fancy clothes or the newest electronic stuff. They'd had what they needed, but not a lot of things they wanted. She hadn't even dated until she went to nursing school because none of the boys at her school wanted to ask her out. Prom had been out of the question—there wasn't money for a fancy dress. Between their regular Joe jobs and her mother's medical expenses, things had always been tight. At least her mother had survived breast cancer, but there'd been a toll taken on the family, and the kids had paid it as well as the adults.

Landon's voice broke through her ruminations. "Babe, you okay?"

"Yeah. It's just that nobody's ever said that to me before. That's all." Was he making fun of her? Trying to get her to believe him when he really didn't mean what he was saying? Being a smartass?

"Then the guys you've been out with are idiots. I think you're the most beautiful thing I've ever seen." There was no taunting in his voice, no mocking, no mirth, just a firmness she found comforting.

"Thank you. I … Thank you."

"You're welcome. Okay." He closed his menu and placed it on the table. "I know what I want. Do you know what you want?"

"Yes." She did the same and clasped her hands together on top of it. "Are we getting wine?"

"If you promise me you'll only have two glasses," he said with a wink.

"Okay. I promise."

"Good. Then yes—wine. Now, on to more important things. Do you go to church somewhere?"

Was this a trick question? "Uh, no. I was raised Baptist, but I don't go."

"I was raised Methodist, but it's not important to me either. Are you a member of any clubs, sororities, things like that?"

"The nursing sorority, but I'm not active. What about you?"

"The firefighters' union. That's about it. Oh, the local rifle and pistol club. Gives me access to the range."

"Got it. Do you play on any teams?"

"Just the firefighters' softball team in the summer. That and the gaming. Oh, and I'm pretty decent at darts. There's a bar across town and we go to the dart tournaments."

"We?"

"Yeah. Me and the guys from the station. We've had self-declared tournaments against the other station houses."

"And?"

He laughed. "Sometimes we win, sometimes we lose. Never know until it's over. But we heckle each other and try to break each other's concentration, so it's pretty funny to watch."

"I bet!"

"So, big family?"

"Eh. My brother and a few cousins. You?"

"My brother and sister. Lots of cousins. My mom was one of thirteen kids. On my dad's side, no. He was an only child."

"Wow! That's pretty different!"

"Yeah. I don't think he's ever gotten used to her big family after all these years!" Landon said with a laugh.

"I can see how that could be!"

"So does all your family live here?"

Jerrica shook her head. "Nah. Some of them live in New Hampshire, and some live in Texas."

Landon's eyes flew open wide. "Texas? That's a long way."

"Yeah. My cousin Elizabeth lives there. They're coming to see us in a few weeks. She's ... Well, I'll tell you that story soon, but it's just a miracle she can come with everything that's happened. But she's got a great guy. His name is Cade. Hey, he's a firefighter too! We should spend some time with them while they're here!"

"Well, yeah! That would be great. What part of Texas?"

"San Antonio."

"Really long way away. But yeah, that sounds like a lot of fun. Maybe we could have a cookout at my house," Landon offered.

"That would be awesome." She stopped dead in her tracks. "Are you sure you'll still want to see me in a few weeks?"

He reached across the table, his hand outstretched, and Jerrica slipped hers into it. She felt warm and safe there with him. The guy was honest and straightforward, and she loved that. "I'm pretty sure I will. Will *you* still want to see *me*?"

"Oh, I'm positive I will. You've already treated me better than anybody has in a long, long time, and this is just our first date." She hoped the smile she gave him conveyed everything she was feeling. God, this couldn't go awry. It was obvious to her that Landon was the guy she'd been looking for over the years, and now that she'd found him, she didn't want to let him go. "I really like you and I want to see where this goes."

"Same here, darlin'. Now, here comes our server, which is a good thing, because I'm starving!" He released her hand to pick up his menu, and she felt the absence of it immediately, like a small hole in her soul.

Landon Fox was it. He was the man of her dreams. How could she worm her way into his heart? All she knew was that she wanted to.

Because he'd already wormed his way into hers.

CHAPTER 4

Dinner went well. Unbelievably, surprisingly well. They were compatible on almost every level. Neither were big TV watchers, preferring to read instead. They did like their movies, though, regardless that he leaned toward action adventure, while she seemed to like chick flicks best. She surprised him when she said she didn't care for shopping. "I don't shop; I buy," she said, which made him hopeful for no Saturday afternoons at the mall. God, he hated that place!

"Think I'll have the dessert quiche," she announced as she downed the last forkful of her sea bass.

"You're going to ruin my surprise then," Landon announced. "I was planning to take you to Gertie's Homemade Pies for dessert."

"Oh, gosh, yes! I love that place! Let's do that!" Jerrica gushed, and he felt like he'd won the lottery. Everything about the evening had been perfect.

"Good. Let's do it. I'll pay the check and we can get out of here." In minutes, they were on their way downtown to the little pie shop.

Landon was sad. It had only taken them about thirty minutes to get and eat their pie, and it was time to go. And he didn't want to. He wanted to stay with her, hold her hand as they walked, talk to her, and just *be* with her. There was no way for her to know how peaceful he felt when her hand was in his. He saw death and destruction every day, and he knew she did too, but as long as they were together, he didn't think about that. All he thought about was her.

The drive back to her place wasn't nearly long enough either, and he thought all the way back about the dilemma he had to face. On one hand, he knew it was way too soon. On the other, he knew she was perfect for him. Taking her to bed was the wrong decision, but walking away was something he wasn't sure he could manage. He parked his truck behind her little car and sat there for a minute, not knowing quite what to do. She roused him from his thoughts when she asked, "Landon? Do you want to come in?"

"Yeah. And that's the problem. I don't just want to come in. I want to stay, and I know I shouldn't."

"Who says you shouldn't? Where's that rule written down?"

Suddenly, he realized she was right. That wasn't written down anywhere. They were grownups; they could make their own rules. And yet he saw that as a commitment, one he didn't take lightly. "You realize, if that happens, I've marked you as mine. I'm not a bed-hopper, baby. I choose my spot and I hunker down. We haven't known each other all that long, and I—"

Those big blue eyes gazed up at him. "Can I tell you a secret?"

Landon nodded. "Sure."

"When I called you that first day? After you brought me home?" He nodded again, then almost came undone when the little pink tip of her tongue slid out from between her lips and wet them. "Your voice. There was something about it. I felt comfortable just listening to you. I wanted to meet you so badly. When the girls said they were going back to that bar, I went because I wanted to see if I could meet you. And when I did … Landon, I was blown away. You were so much more than I'd fantasized about. Everything about you is perfect for me. Please, don't go?"

God, when she puts it that way, how can I refuse? Landon reached for Jerrica's hand and gripped it tight. "You want to be mine?"

She gave him a single, decisive nod. "I do. And I want you to be mine."

"Then I have something I have to insist on."

She giggled. "Okay. What's that?"

"You go in, get your things, and come to my house. I don't want to be able to get up and leave you, and I don't want you to be able to get up and leave me. If we do that, I have to bring you home and I have nowhere to go. We're stuck with each other. Does that make sense?"

She looked down at her lap and sighed. "Yeah. There's nothing worse than waking up to find out the person you were with the night before has sneaked out and left you without so much as a goodbye."

"Exactly. That's not going to happen here. We lie down together, we get up together. No compromise on that one. Can you deal with that?"

"Let me get a bag and throw some things in. I'll let you bring me home to shower and change before work tomorrow."

"Sounds good to me. Let's go." He watched with delight as she sat in the truck and waited for him to come around and open her door. "Come on, beautiful. Let's get you packed."

It only took her about ten minutes to get everything she thought she needed and they were back in his truck. He was almost home when he remembered something. "Hang on. I've got to make a stop." Cutting the wheels on the truck, he roared into the drug store parking lot. "Be right back."

There had to be a hundred different kinds of condoms sitting there on the shelves. How in the hell could he choose? *Pre-lubricated and ribbed for her pleasure*. Yeah, that sounded like a good choice. He almost told the clerk to forget about the bag and let him carry them out until he realized that might be uncomfortable for Jerrica, so he let her bag them and headed out the door.

"What was that about?" Landon handed her the bag and slipped his key into the ignition as she looked inside. "Oh."

"Yeah. Didn't have any at home and thought I'd better grab some."

"That's awfully presumptuous of you," she said, but when he turned to say something snarky, he caught the mischief in her eyes. "Just kidding."

"I was about to say that I don't usually purchase a whole box of condoms unless I'm pretty sure I'm going to need them."

She giggled. "The whole box?"

"Well, yeah! There's only twenty-four in there! How long do you think that's gonna last?" It was his turn to give her a devilish grin when she caught his eye. "Okay, maybe I'm being a little overly optimistic, but I'm hoping I'll need more than a couple."

It got quiet in the truck's cab, but in a few minutes she finally spoke. "You know, this is hot."

"What?"

"Knowing what we're about to do. I mean, it's not like we're guessing. I know exactly what you're thinking, you know exactly what I'm thinking, and we're headed there to do it right now. That's pretty damn hot."

"Yeah, I guess it is. But I thought you were concerned with spontaneity."

Jerrica laughed aloud. "This is more like Disneyworld. I know I'm going and I can't wait to get there!"

"I see what you mean! But I tend to not beat around the bush about things."

"I hope you do some beating around the bush tonight," she snapped back.

"Whole different bush, baby. Whole different bush. Okay, here we are." The truck rolled to a stop in his driveway and he cut the engine. "You're sure you're ready for this?"

"As ready as you are."

Landon snickered. "Oh, I sincerely doubt that."

"Oh yeah? I guess we'll find out, won't we?"

Landon rounded the front end of the truck and opened her door. Instead of waiting for her to get out, he clamped his hands around her waist and lifted her, then set her on the ground in front of him. In the process, he got a whiff of something.

Her arousal. It was a sweet, warm, musky scent that filled the air around them, and Landon's knees went weak. She really *did* want him as much as he wanted her, and he could feel himself hardening with the knowledge. Walking was going to be difficult with a tree trunk in the front of his slacks, but he'd manage, he was sure. As he reached into his pocket for his keys, he wrapped his other arm around her from behind and pulled her back against him. There was no doubt in his mind that she could feel his concrete-hard dick against the cleft of her ass, and that was exactly what he wanted. "Here we go," he whispered into her ear as the door swung open.

The door had barely closed behind him when she wheeled on him and pinned him up against its smooth coolness with her hands on either side of his waist. Landon's hands came up to cradle her face and pull it toward his, and when his lips reached hers, he latched on with a ferociousness that surprised even him. In seconds, he'd spun her and she was the one trapped against the door as his mouth ravaged hers. His hands slid up and down her back, feeling the hooks on the band of her bra and wondering if he was still talented enough to undo them with one hand. There was a tugging sensation and she lifted his shirt, so he just unbuttoned it and dropped it on the floor. "Oh, Jesus, look at you," Jerrica whispered into his lips.

"I want to look at you," he whispered back and reached down to the hem of her dress. As soon as it was up and off, he looked down at her. Two perfect breasts swelled above the demi cups of her bra, and her little lace thong matched perfectly. He couldn't speak. All he could do was meld himself to her again, feeling the lace of the undergarment rub against his chest. Fuck, he wanted her, wanted her so badly, and he couldn't think, just feel. His kisses were hard and insistent, and he worried that he'd bruise her lips, but she was returning every stroke with her own. Breaking away, he grabbed her hand. "Come on. Do whatever you need to do to freshen up and let's get on with this, shall we?"

"Yes. Let's." Her voice was breathy and stilted, and he knew she was as turned on as he was. "I'll only be a minute." Pulling her into the bedroom with him, he pointed at the door and she disappeared into the bathroom.

Landon headed up the hallway to the guest bath. There was a brand new toothbrush in the drawer that he'd gotten from the dentist and a tiny tube of toothpaste from the same visit. As soon as he'd brushed his teeth, he splashed water on his face, jumped in the shower to rinse off, and padded back to the bedroom with nothing but a towel wrapped around his waist.

She was still in the bathroom, so he dropped the towel and crawled under the sheet. As he lay there waiting, he thought about the scent of her perfume and the softness of her skin. God, he couldn't wait to take her, to make her his, and to enjoy their bodies together. He thought he was prepared when she stepped out of the bathroom.

He was not. His heart almost skidded to a stop when he took in those two round, pert breasts, their nipples hard and rosy, and the smooth strip of hair on her mound. One second his mouth was dry and it was hard to swallow, and the next, he was drooling. She stepped to the side of the bed and stood there for a second. "Mind if I join you?"

"Not at all. Please," he answered with what he hoped

was a sexy smile. She slid into the bed and scooted close to him. "Know what I want to do first?"

"Oh, I can't imagine, firefighter," she whispered to him.

"I just want to hold you. I want to feel you against me, your skin against mine, the warmth of your body. Is that weird?"

"No. I think it's sweet, and I'd love that." Landon held out an arm and in seconds, he felt her mold herself to his side, her breasts pressed into him and her hand draped across his waist. Her cheek was feather light on his chest. "Oh, this is nice," she murmured as he kissed her forehead.

"Yeah, it is, isn't it? You're so soft and warm, babe. I could hold you like this all night, but I think there are more pressing matters to attend to."

"Oh, yeah? Like what?"

"Like this." Pressing her away and flat onto her back, he leaned down and kissed her as his hands roamed her body. When he pinched a nipple between his finger and thumb, she gasped into his mouth and her back arched. He worked first one and then the other, listening to her breath hitch and the occasional moan that slipped from her lips. Replacing his hand with his mouth, he sucked in a hardened bud and pulled, drawing an even louder moan from her. His hand wandered to her other nipple and teased it mercilessly as he sucked and nipped, listening to her breathing change.

"Oh, god, Landon, I want to see you." Her breath came out as a raspy wheeze.

"You will, baby. Right now we've got business to attend to." *Thank god I've got long arms,* he chided himself as he thrust an arm under her and wrapped it around her torso to tease her left nipple as he sucked on the right, and his right hand wandered downward. As soon as it reached her mound, he balled up his fist and massaged the flesh there with his knuckles.

"Oh, god! Landon! Oh, that's … Yeah, so good, babe." That almost made him chuckle. Most men had no idea how sensitive that little pad of flesh was, but he knew, and he used it to his advantage. But that wasn't enough. It wasn't nearly enough.

And so his fingers wandered farther down until he found her slit. Dipping his finger into her, he found her slick and ready, and his cock hardened even more. She wanted him, that much was plain, and the aroma of her arousal struck him again. It was light and fragrant but still ridiculously potent, and it had the power to leave him breathless.

But he wasn't breathless. He owned her body. Lips on one nipple, fingers torturing the other, and his free hand finding her clit, he began to slowly and methodically stroke the tiny bundle of nerves, listening to her cry out and feeling her squirm under him. He lifted his head ever so slightly and whispered, "Come on, baby. Turn loose. I know you want to. I want to see you come apart, Jerrica. Come for me, babe. I know you can."

"Oh, god, Landon … Yeah, right there. A little to the left, ohhhhhh … My god, you're, yeah, ohhhh … A little faster, baby, please? Just a little? Uh-huh, just like that. Oh, yeah, Landon, make me come, baby. Make me … AHHHHHH!" she screamed as she bucked and shook. He wasn't sure how much she could stand so he kept going until she cried out, "Oh, god, stop! No more! No more!"

Instead of releasing her instantly, he leaned over and kissed her mound, then began kissing all the way up her torso. Holy fuck, she was beautiful, her chest heaving from his ministrations and her hands winding through her own hair, pulling upward as she fought the ecstasy he'd given her. When he reached the hollow at her collarbone, he gave it a quick suck and listened to her breath hitch again before he reached for a condom, ripped the package open, and rolled it on. There was no need to question if she was ready for him—her legs opened and he slipped between them like he belonged there. "Baby?" When she didn't answer, he said, "Jerrica?"

"Yeah?"

"This means something to me, darlin'. When I enter you, that's my pact with you. Do you understand?"

Her eyes popped open, she lifted her head just a little, and she smiled. "I feel the same way, Landon. I want you inside me so bad."

That was all the encouragement he needed, and when the head of his shaft breached her entrance, she wasn't the only one who groaned. He was no virgin, but he couldn't remember a woman feeling tighter or hotter or more perfect around him than she did. "Babe, stroke yourself. Do it, Jerrica. I want to feel you pulse around me, babe. Please?"

He didn't have to tell her twice, and in seconds, she roared into her second orgasm as he picked up the pace from stroking to pounding. The power he felt was incredible, but not nearly as powerful as he felt when he watched her back arch and felt her muscles massage him through the condom. His strokes grew frantic and when she let out a low, guttural groan, he knew she was coming again, but that time it would be purely from his length inside her. She gripped his forearms, bore down, and cried out with joy just as Landon's body gave up its fight and emptied into the latex.

He dropped on top of her and wrapped his arms around her, his head face down beside hers on the pillow. *MY woman,* he told himself as he tightened his grip around her. *She belongs with me.*

Her voice was tiny when she whispered, "Landon?"

"Yeah, babe?"

"I know it's too soon, but I think I'm falling in love with you."

He wanted to cry. He wanted to dance. The joy he felt was indescribable. Rising up on his elbows above her, he looked down and smiled into her face. "I think I'm falling in love with you too."

"Guess we'll have to do this until we're sure, huh?" she asked and whisked a strand of hair out of her eyes.

"Guess so. We'll do it again in a few minutes. Right now, let's nap a little, whaddya say? I ate too much dinner and I feel like I'm going to fall asleep right here on top of you!"

"You're too heavy for that!" she said, laughing as he rolled off and beside her.

"I'm too heavy?" he mocked.

"Nah. Actually, you're just right. I felt safe with your weight on top of me, like you were covering me and protecting me from the rest of the world."

"I want to always be the one to protect you from the world, darlin'. I want that to be my number one job, that and to always make you feel like you have a place to run to."

She snuggled into his chest. "I have a place to run to. It's your arms."

"As long as you remember that, we'll all be okay." Landon dropped a soft little kiss on her forehead and sighed. It was real. She was there with him. And he was never, never letting her go.

* * *

What was that crazy noise? It took Landon a couple of seconds for it to make sense, and he realized it was something in the drawer. His phone. It had quit buzzing, but the screen said he'd missed a call from Juice. His left arm was still wrapped around Jerrica, and he managed to extricate himself without waking her, then tiptoed out into the hallway to call him back. *Three twenty-three in the morning. This had better be good,* he groused to himself. "Okay, man, what the hell?"

"Shit, boy, go get your turnout gear and get down here. They're calling everybody in."

"What? Where? What's going on?"

"Big one this time, man. You know that old shoe factory building?" Landon felt a groan coming on. "Damn thing's blazing. It'll take the rest of the block with it. They're calling in all the volunteer units from all the counties around here to help. Captain said get your ass on the phone and get you down here."

"Okay. I'll be there as fast as I can get there. Thanks." Landon ended the call and stood there for a second, thinking about Jerrica as she lay there in his bed.

He'd no more than rounded the door jamb when she asked, her voice groggy from sleep, "What's going on?"

"Huge fire downtown. I've gotta go. Want me to take you home?"

"What time is it?"

"About three thirty."

"I don't have to go in until afternoon. But you shouldn't go, baby. You've still got a concussion and—"

"I don't have a choice. This is a bad situation, and they're calling everybody in."

Jerrica buried her face in her pillow and groaned. "Go. Go on. I'll be fine."

"Babe, I'm sorry. I—"

"Hey, I get it. It's no biggie. At least I know you're not running off to another woman," she said with a weak giggle.

"Nope." He knelt with one knee on the mattress and bent down over her. "This is killing me, leaving you here like this. I'll be back as soon as I can."

"I know. Please, be careful?"

"You know I will. Bye, babe." He carried his clothes out of the room with him and closed the door behind him, then dressed in the living room. The sooner she could get to sleep, the better.

But it looked like the sleep he'd already gotten was all the sleep he was going to get.

* * *

"We're taxing the water lines! There's not enough water pressure!"

"Get that tank truck on the road!" Landon yelled to two of the guys, and they turned and hot-footed it toward the big rig. "We need more water—NOW!"

Captain Martin appeared at his left. "You got enough men?"

"Yeah, but not enough water. I think we're about to

exhaust the water tower, and when that happens, I don't know what we'll do."

"That tanker truck should help, but we've got an awful lot of water running," the captain said.

"Yeah, and it's not doing any good. At this point, looks like it would be best to contain it and let it burn. There's so much flammable shit in there that we'll never put this out."

"And that's your best advice?"

"Yes, sir."

Without asking, the captain removed the radio from Landon's hand. "All Station Two personnel, all Station Two personnel, stand down. Our unit is to treat this as containment, not suppression. Repeat, containment, not suppression." Landon could feel it—there was a shift in the area, and he saw firefighters who'd been seemingly absent for a couple of hours start to reappear, grabbing a drink of water or mopping their brows and the backs of their necks with cold, wet cloths, then dropping their buckets back on their heads and getting back to the job. He listened with pride as he heard the captains of the other houses instruct their men in the same tactic. They'd taken the lead, and it seemed everyone else was willing to follow.

It was midday. They'd been there all night, and they'd lost a lot. Three firefighters had been taken to the hospital, none with life-threatening injuries, and yet they were there. Hell, Landon wasn't even supposed to be there, but he'd gone anyway. It seemed the captain had suddenly remembered that when he said, "Hose, what the hell are you doing here anyway?"

"Juice called me and told me what was going on, that you were calling everybody in. I guess he didn't even think about it, just made the call. Honestly, I didn't think about it either, just pulled on my clothes and got in my truck. I'm glad I did. We needed everybody tonight."

"Hell, we've got firefighters from Hardin County here. That's pretty damn far away. This could've been a lot worse," Captain Martin replied, standing beside Landon and watching the flames. "But you proved yourself tonight. I watched these guys. They followed your lead and did exactly what you told them to, and to them, you're just another one of the guys. They don't even know about your promotion. Fox, you're a natural-born leader. Don't ever let anybody tell you otherwise."

"Thank you, sir. I just see what needs to be done and do it. That's all."

"And that works. Good work, lieutenant. Take a break and sit down. You've earned it."

"Thank you, sir." Landon watched the captain walk away and smiled. It was nice to have hard work acknowledged, and he knew a lot of the other captains weren't like that. But Captain Martin inspired courage and teamwork, and he respected that.

As soon as he sat down on the curb with a bottle of water, he pulled out his phone and made the call. He could hear the fear in her voice when she answered. "God, babe, I've been so worried! Are you okay?"

"Yeah, I'm fine, but this building isn't. It's going to collapse in about an hour and we're in the process of getting everybody backed away from it. You okay?"

"Yeah, just worried, that's all."

"What time do you have to go in?'

"Four."

"I'll be there in time to pick you up and take you to your place. And Jerrica?"

"Yeah?"

He took a deep breath. "Leaving you this morning was the hardest thing I've ever done. I just want to feel you in my arms again."

"Lying in your arms is my new favorite pastime, Landon Fox. I need you."

"I need you too. I'll be there as soon as I can."

"Okay. Bye."

"Bye, baby." He ended the call and held the edge of the phone to his lips, deep in thought. He'd almost said *I love you*. Did he? Yeah, he thought he did. But it would be best to hang onto that until he was sure, of course. Best not to drag that out and parade it around if he wasn't yet certain.

Downing the last of the water, he dropped the bottle into a barrel nearby and trotted up to a police officer. "We need to start moving the perimeter out. This building will topple in about an hour, and we can't have anybody as close as they are, especially not them," he said and pointed toward the growing crowd of media outlets clogging the sidewalk just yards away.

"Yes, sir. We'll start moving everybody back. I'll tell my captain. Who can I say gave the order?"

"Lieutenant Fox from Station Two." It felt good to be able to say that.

"Yes, sir." With that, the officer jogged away toward a cluster of vehicles and Landon went back toward the fire.

"Station Two, Station Two, clear the area. Containment complete—clear the structure. I repeat, clear the structure." He could hear his guys out there, echoing his command, and he watched as one firefighter after another began to move away from the smoldering hulk, still spraying water but making sure they were far enough out that a wall couldn't hit them.

It only took another forty-five minutes before the first wall fell, and then the second. The third took the fourth with it, and old bricks rained down onto the street, but all of the firefighters were out of the way. One got hit in the shin as a brick bounced, but that was all, and Landon was relieved. No one else had gotten hurt, and now they could go in and finish putting the fire completely out. He caught Stingray as the younger man was headed toward the first responder unit to get a bottle of drinking water. "Hey, got an errand to run, but I'll be right back, okay?"

"Sure. We've got this. See you in a few."

"Roger that." Landon jogged toward his truck and in seconds, he was on the road.

"Holy shit," Jerrica breathed as he walked into the house. "You're suited up."

"Yeah. Full turnout gear. Didn't have time to change, and I'm going back after I take you home. Come on—let's go. I've gotta get back."

"Sure! Just a second. Let me grab my things." In under a minute, she was ready to go.

They drove along and, to Landon's surprise, it wasn't awkward at all. He felt like a guy taking his long-time girlfriend somewhere. "Sheesh, you smell like musty old smoke. So, was it really bad?" she asked.

"Really bad. The old shoe factory."

"Oh, god! All that junk inside it!"

"Yeah. Lots of canvas and leather. Plenty of fuel. Whatever happened there, it was the perfect storm fire-wise."

"Did anybody get hurt?"

"Three guys went to the hospital, but they weren't serious injuries. Just better to be safe than sorry."

"Exactly. I'm surprised they let you come down there, what with your concussion."

"Babe, there were firefighters from Hardin County here."

Jerrica's mouth dropped open. "Hardin County? Elizabethtown?"

"Yep. All over. Downtown Taylorsville looks like a firefighting convention."

"My god. Is it out?"

"Not completely, but the building collapsed."

"That's bad!"

"No, that's good. Nothing left for us to be hurt by. Now we can just concentrate on putting out hot spots and getting the whole thing down."

"Oh. That makes sense." He pulled up in front of her little duplex and parked the truck. "You don't have to—"

"Yes. I do." In seconds, the door was open and he was helping her down, then took her bag and carried it for her.

Once the door was unlocked and open, she turned to him. "I suppose you can't stay."

"No. I can't. But I can stay long enough for this." He stepped in, closed the door behind him, and swept her up in his arms to kiss her. When he finished, he chuckled. "*Now* I have to go!"

"Okay. Be careful and send me a text when you're home and safe, please?"

"I'll do it. Bye, babe. See you soon."

"Bye."

Landon marched out to the truck, got in, and drove away. For the second time on that calendar date, he felt like he was going to die if he didn't turn around and run right back to her, but he couldn't. If they were together for fifty years, would that feeling ever fade?

God, he hoped not!

* * *

"Fox!"

Landon jumped up and ran toward the captain's office. "Yes, sir?"

"Sit down." As soon as he was in a chair, the captain reared back in his own and smiled. "Your ceremony is set for the twenty-third of this month. That's three weeks from now. The department will provide you with forty engraved invitations to mail out. We'll also do the cake and soft drinks. Anything else you want, you or your family can provide."

"Yes, sir. Thank you, sir. I don't have forty people to invite, but I'll see if I can come up with—"

"Landon?"

"Yes, sir?"

"I know what you're thinking. And you may be right—they may not show up. But give them the benefit of the doubt and at least invite them. They might surprise you."

Landon's shoulders slumped and he let out a long sigh. "Yes, sir. But I already know—"

"Benefit of the doubt, lieutenant."

"Yes, sir."

"Okay, then. We good?"

"Yes, sir."

"Good. The twenty-third. Tell them soon so they can put it on their calendars. Damn doctors never have time for anything family-related, but they can sure find time for golf," Captain Martin said with a sneer.

"Yes, sir. Thank you, sir. Anything else?"

"Just good work on the shoe factory fire."

"Thank you, sir."

"You're welcome. You earned the praise. Don't make me regret it."

Landon laughed. "Yes, sir!"

His promotion ceremony was on the twenty-third. He had a lot to do, and two of the most important things would be the hardest.

* * *

He shot her a quick text: *Meet me at Blue Moon?*

Sure. I don't get off until ten.

That's fine. I'll be there waiting. XOXO

Can't wait! XOXO

So she'd be there at ten. They had a lot to talk about, and Landon was getting a little excited. If he could manage it all before the ceremony, maybe there was a chance that things would be good. Stingray, Juice, and Rodeo were already there when he got there. Stingray was the first to ask. "Where have you been?"

"Home. Doing laundry."

"Laundry? Why aren't you down here looking for stray tail?" Rodeo wanted to know.

"I don't have to look. I've got somebody."

Juice shook his head. "Don't tell us it's the drunk chick."

"She's not a drunk chick. She just had a little too much that night, that was all. She's fine."

"Whatever you say, man. Hey, I heard a rumor that there's going to be a press conference on Monday. They're going to name somebody to Speedy's job, is that right?" Speedy was their former lieutenant, and he'd been killed in a motorcycle crash.

"'Bout time," Rodeo piped up. "That slot's been empty for a while. Any idea who?"

Juice shook his head. "Nope. They're playing it close to the vest, but it's gotta be one of our guys. Shame it's not you, Hose Jockey."

What the hell should he do? He didn't want to lie to his best friends! "Um, I can neither confirm nor deny." Three heads swiveled his direction. "And that's all I can say."

"Whaaaaa? Are you serious? And you didn't tell us?" Stingray almost yelled.

"There's nothing to tell. I can neither confirm nor deny," Landon repeated.

"You dog! How long have you known?" Rodeo asked.

"I can neither confirm nor deny."

"Cut the bullshit," Juice barked.

Landon shook his head. "Nope. Sworn to secrecy."

"Well, if it is you, congratulations," Rodeo said. "And if it's not, shame on you for making us think it is."

"Sorry, guys." He looked up just in time to see a small cluster of women step into the bar, and Jerrica was among them. "And now I must say my goodbyes. M'lady awaits."

"Pussy whipped already," he heard Stingray mutter from behind him. Jealous bastard. He'd get over it.

He wanted desperately to kiss her, but instead, he just took her hand. "Hey, baby."

"Hey yourself! Where are we?"

"Let's take this booth back here. We've got some things to talk about."

"Oh? Sounds serious," she said as she scooted in.

"It is, kinda. Not serious-serious, just serious." Once he was seated, he motioned to the server. "She'll have a glass of merlot and I'll have another one of these," he said, tapping on his mug. "Now, what we need to talk about," he started as the server walked away. "My promotion ceremony is the twenty-third."

"Not much time, huh?"

"No. They'll provide invitations, the cake, and soft drinks. I'd really like to do a little more. You know, maybe finger sandwiches or something like that."

Jerrica chuckled. "You sound like you know a thing or two about throwing a party!"

"I worked for a caterer when I was in high school, so yeah—I do know a bit. And I think that's doable. Would you … maybe …"

"Make them?"

"Gosh, no! I was just wondering if you'd coordinate

it and take care of getting it together. No, I don't want you doing something like that when I can easily pay for it instead. I want it to be fun for you too. I want you …" He stopped dead.

"What?"

"I want you …" *Out with it, Fox!* he scolded himself. "I want you to be the hostess that day, if you'll do it."

"Oh, god, I'd *love* to do that for you! No problem! Consider it done!"

"Great. Now for the thing we need to talk about."

Jerrica's eyes went wide. "That wasn't it?"

"Oh, no. Not at all. There are two things I've got to do before this shindig takes place. One is introduce you to my parents and try to get them to come. And the other—"

"Meet mine."

Landon nodded. "Yep. I'd like to invite them too, if they want to come."

"I can tell you my dad will want to be there, and my mom will too."

"What about your brother?"

"His gaming buddy is being promoted? Try to stop him from being there!" Jerrica said and laughed.

"Okay. That's settled. I'll get the invitations and we can figure out who to send them to. Now, in more current news, we were supposed to have a get-together this weekend. Still want to do that?"

"Sure! It'll be fun. I'd like to meet all your friends

when they aren't hitting on my friends, if you know what I mean."

"Good. Sounds like a plan. We'll have them all over and pray that nothing happens while we're holding the party."

Jerrica sighed. "You didn't get much sleep last night."

"I got almost no sleep last night. And I woke you, which I'm sorry for."

"Oh, no biggie. But you need some rest. Shift tomorrow?"

"No. Two more days on my disabled list status. That's what the captain said."

"Yeah. Smart man." Jerrica cuffed his chin affectionately. "You really should take it easy. I'm surprised they let you be there today."

"It was such a mess that they needed everybody they could get."

Jerrica propped her elbows on the table and rested her chin in her hands. "So what's going on with these fires downtown?"

"Good question. Something, that's for sure. These are buildings that have no electricity or gas run to them, so there's really nothing in there to catch fire. The fire marshal's been looking them over but, so far, he can't determine what's happened to them."

"That's a shame. But hey, at least they aren't inhabited, right?"

"There's always a chance a homeless person is living

in them. That could mean a death if they couldn't get out," Landon pointed out.

"True. Maybe somebody will come up with something soon. As for meeting my parents, you don't think it's too soon?"

Landon shrugged. "Do you?"

"Not really."

"Then I'm game."

"What about me meeting yours?"

He sucked in a breath and blew it out. "*That* may be a bit harder. You'll have to be prepared—they'll take a swipe at me with everything they have. They can't help themselves. And don't take up for me in front of them. Let me handle them. I know it'll be tempting, but don't do it. If my dad thinks you're being 'insolent,' you'll never last in my family. That's one of their biggest beefs with me."

"I'll sit there and keep my mouth shut, although I want you to know I'll want to say something."

Landon patted her arm. "I know, babe, and I appreciate it."

"You're welcome. So let's plan this party. Do you want to grill, or should we buy meat, or …" As they talked and laughed, Landon felt better about the whole situation.

Okay, just a little better, but he'd take what he could get.

CHAPTER 5

Jerrica stood on the patio at Landon's house, encircled by the biggest group of buff guys she'd ever seen and enough testosterone to power a small city. "Okay, let me see if I've got it. Stingray, Juice, Rodeo," she said, pointing to Landon's friends, "Bongo, Frenchy, Mater, Bobo, Spooky, Red, and, um … Don't tell me … Tinman!"

"That was good!" Stingray sang out. "I can't believe you remembered them all!"

"Thank god there aren't more of you or I wouldn't be able to!" Jerrica said, laughing. Betsy and Mina had to work, but Jolie, Brandy, and Megan had come. She'd made it clear to them that it was *not* supposed to be a gathering for them to find guys to hook up with, just something light and fun, and the girls had agreed to tone it down a bit. Unfortunately, Landon hadn't had the same talk with the guys, and several of them had made plays. The only ones with any success had been Pete, Lucas, and Hayes, and only because the girls already knew them. They were all friendly, but it didn't look to Jerrica like they'd be leaving together.

"You do know what his nickname is, don't you?" Juice asked and pointed at Landon.

"Yeah, he told me."

"Did he tell you the story behind it?" Rodeo asked her. When she shook her head, he laughed. "Hose, I can't believe you didn't fill her in!"

"I didn't want to embarrass myself like that, but I have a feeling you'll be glad to do it for me!" Landon said, laughing.

"Who's gonna tell it?" Rodeo asked.

"I guess I will. I was there." Stingray made a big production out of sitting up straight. "Okay, so we were at a training. We were all rookies, and we were all struggling. There was a hose on the ground, and they were showing us how to handle it correctly. And one of the instructors said, 'You'll be surprised at the force of one of these things when we turn it on.' So we took turns, one at a time. When it was Hose's turn, he took the nozzle, but he was standing with one foot on either side of the hose. He had hold of it, but when they turned it on, BAM! It popped up and hit him right in the family jewels!" The other guys roared with laughter.

Jerrica made a face. "Owwww!"

"Yeah, he was all doubled over and groaning, and

we were all laughing, and the instructor said, 'Always know where your feet are. Being a hose jockey isn't a good idea.' Oh my god, it was so funny! And that's where he got the name."

"*I* didn't think it was funny," Landon said with a smirk on his face.

"Neither did your future children!" Tinman said and the group howled with laughter again.

"Yeah, yeah. There's a funny story behind pretty much every one of your names, so don't get me started. Hey, babe, isn't it dessert time?" Landon asked, grinning at Jerrica.

"It is! All kinds of desserts are on the sideboard in there, and dishes and forks too. Help yourselves." She watched as every guy in the group hustled toward their own personal little food nirvana.

A pair of strong arms wrapped around her from behind. "Thank you for this. I think everybody's having a good time," Landon whispered in her ear.

She patted his forearms. "You're welcome. I'm having a good time too. I'm just thankful the girls helped me with some of the food. This is quite a crowd!"

"At least they're not climbing the guys' legs tonight."

"Yeah, no kidding. This is much more relaxed than providing a dating service with dinner," Jerrica said with a laugh.

Landon headed to the door, then turned. "Want something? I'll bring you anything you ask for."

"You. On a silver platter."

He laughed. "Oh, you'll get that, baby. Just wait 'til they're gone!"

* * *

"No. No slacks. Jeans."

"But I want to look nice!"

"I want you to look nice, but I also don't want you to intimidate them. My parents are plain people. My dad will be in jeans and a tee-shirt, I can promise you. That would be best for you to wear."

"Really?" She nodded. "Well, okay then. Tee and jeans it is."

"And your athletic shoes."

"Okay. Anything else?"

"No. The rest should be fine. This has got to be super casual."

"Got it." Landon redressed and looked in the mirror. Yeah, he looked okay. It felt funny, going to meet somebody's parents and dressing down, but if that was what she thought best, that's what he'd do.

They pulled up five minutes early on Wednesday night and Landon helped Jerrica out of the truck. When they got to the front door, Jerrica stuck her head in and yelled, "Mom! Dad! We're here!"

"Oh, my goodness! You're early! Come on in!" a female voice called back. A woman in her late fifties appeared in the hallway, small but curvy, wiping her hands on her apron. "Hi, honey!" she said and hugged Jerrica, then turned to Landon. "And you must be the young man we've heard so much about!"

"Yes, ma'am, Mrs. Ligon."

"That's Amy to you. Jeffrey, Landon is here!"

The man who joined them was about the same age as the woman, but taller and tanned. There wasn't an extra ounce of fat anywhere on him. "Well, hello there! Glad to finally meet you."

"And you too, sir."

"Ah, it's just Jeff. And you're Landon, right? Come on in! Want a beer?"

"Sure! That would be great." He followed Jeff into what appeared to be a den.

"Just have a seat. Oh, thank you, baby," Jeff said to Jerrica as she handed him and Landon both a bottle of beer, then headed back to the kitchen to help her mother. "So, Jerrica says you're a firefighter."

"Yes, sir, I am."

"No sir. Just Jeff. That's not necessary. We're all friends here."

"Then yes, I'm a firefighter. Station Two."

"Oh! Over on Birch Street! Yeah, one of the newer ones. Lucky you. Hey, those fires downtown, they're awful."

"Yeah, we buried one of my fellow firefighters the other day."

"I heard about that. Jerrica said you were hurt at the same time."

"I've got staples in my head and I had a concussion."

"So, tell me, where did you meet my daughter?"

"At a local hangout. My friends and I go there after work sometimes, and she and some of her friends came in. That's how we got to know each other."

"Did she tell you about Dusty?"

"Is that her brother?"

"No, no. Dusty is—"

"Daddy? Landon? Mom's putting dinner on the table. Are Liam and Darlene coming?"

Her father seemed perturbed. "They'll be here. They're always late. Jerrica, why haven't you told Landon about—"

"Come on. Let's eat. There'll be plenty of time to talk later." Before Landon knew what was happening, Jerrica had him by the arm, hustling him into the tiny dining room. They'd barely had time to sit down before a large figure loomed in the doorway. "There you are! Liam, Darlene, this is my friend, Landon. Landon, my brother and his wife."

Landon stood and reached a hand out to Liam. "Good to finally meet you, DozerBrother."

Her brother's jaw dropped. "How did you know my gaming name?"

Landon grinned. "HoseJockey."

"Holy shit! You're kidding me! How did you two meet?" Liam shook Landon's hand enthusiastically and his eyes lit up. "This is great! I never get to meet any of my gaming partners in person!"

"Fluke, actually. I mentioned gaming, she told me your gaming name, and there it was. It's great to meet you too. And you're the first of my gaming partners that I've met."

"Small world, isn't it, boys?" Amy asked with a wide smile. "Everybody, sit down and let's eat!"

Food was passed, sweet tea and soft drinks flowed, and everyone enjoyed themselves. When they were finished eating, Jeff invited Landon out to the garage to look at his vintage car. The body and interior of the old Mustang were in great shape, and he'd been working on it in his spare time over the last two years, trying to get it running. "This is awesome, Jeff. I mean, really. It looks amazing."

"Thanks. I do a little here and there when I can afford it. Restoration is expensive." He stopped, and Landon could tell he wanted to say something. "Has Jerrica told you about Dusty?"

"No. Is this something for Jerrica to talk to me about?" Landon asked. He didn't want to have that conversation with Jeff if it was something that should be left to Jerrica.

"All I can tell you is that Dusty's dead. For the whole story, she needs to tell you. Hell, she needs to talk about it. She avoids it like the plague, but she needs to get it all out, especially if the two of you are embarking on a relationship. Honestly, I'm surprised she'd take up with a firefighter. I figured that would be way out of her comfort zone, seeing as how you're in danger all the time."

"Well, not *all* the time. We do a fair amount of, for lack of a better term, public relations. Cats in trees, elderly people who fall and can't get up. We see all kinds of things. Fires aren't something we see every day."

"Lately that doesn't seem to be the case," Jeff pointed out.

Landon nodded his bowed head. "Yeah. It's been crazy. I hope we figure out what's going on pretty soon. It's about to get out of hand."

"I'd say it already has. But please, be good to my little girl and don't put yourself at unnecessary risk. Losing a second boyfriend might be more than she can stand."

"I'll do everything I can to come home to her every night, Mr. Ligon."

"That's Jeff."

"In this instance, no. It's Mr. Ligon. You have my word I'll always be there for her unless it's beyond my control."

"Fair enough. We should go back inside. She's going to be mad at me as it is," Jeff said with a wink.

The evening had gone extremely well, and Amy even hugged Landon as they were leaving. "Come back soon," she ordered.

"I'll do that! Thanks for dinner. It was great." He

waved as he helped Jerrica into her seat, then climbed in on his side and took off. "That was fun."

"Yeah, my family is great. We're not rich, but we love each other, we get along, and we do what we can to help one another."

"That's what really matters." Even as he spoke, he was thinking about what Jeff had told him. How could he get it out of her? "Your dad's Mustang is amazing. He's done a great job with it."

"Cut the crap, Landon. I know he took you out there and talked to you about Dusty."

That left him with nothing to say. He fished around in his brain for a few seconds, but what he came up with was, "He told me you'd tell me."

"Oh, he did, did he? I guess he's left me no choice now."

"Is it so bad that you don't want me to know?"

"No. It's so bad that I don't really want to talk about it, but I have to. Shit. Okay." She stopped and took a deep breath, then blew it out. "Dusty hung himself."

Landon almost tromped on the brake pedal in surprise. "What?"

"He hung himself. From a tree branch. On my twenty-fifth birthday."

"And how long had you been together?"

"Since we were thirteen."

No wonder it had been hard for her to talk about. "Were you planning to get married?"

"We talked about it all the time, but he was an addict. I told him I wouldn't marry him until he had his addiction under control. He'd gone off to rehab half a dozen times and came back every time to start using again. He was so high at my birthday party that he fell on the table and ruined the cake. I told him to get out and not come back until he cleaned himself up for good."

"And later that night ..."

"Yeah. Later that night. His dad found him. They blamed me for being so tough on him. I blamed them for enabling him. They didn't even want me at his funeral. Twelve years of my life, gone in a flash at the end of a rope, and everybody's mad at me. Well, everybody but my family. They understood. My parents were sick of it because it was making me sick." She stopped for a few seconds, sighed, and said, "And that's the story of Dusty."

In that moment, he understood why she'd been drinking the night he met her. That guilt, heaped onto her by others for doing what she had to do to survive, had eaten at her. Landon decided it would stop that very instant. "You realize none of that was your fault."

"I know that in here," she said and pointed to her head, then folded her hand over her chest right above her left breast. "But it doesn't feel that way in here. In here, I feel like the worst person in the world."

"But you're not. You couldn't let him drag you down with him, honey. That would've wasted two lives."

"I know. But you know what? When I'm with you I feel whole, Landon. It's like all of that was a bad dream and I've finally awakened from it. It's heaven for me."

"I'm glad I'm good for something!" he said, laughing.

Jerrica snuggled into his shoulder as he drove. "You're good for me."

"Then my mission is complete. By the way, I'm taking you to your place, but I'd love it if you'd come home with me."

"Tell you what. I've got laundry in the washer. Let me get it in the dryer and finished and I'll drive out. How's that?"

"Perfect. I'll stop along the way and get us some snacks."

Three hours later as he surged into her for the second time, Landon filled the condom and stilled on top of Jerrica. Her arms encircled his waist and she squeezed. "Ohhh, that feels good," he moaned, rising up on his elbows to kiss her. The kiss went on and on as he rolled them to their sides and his softening manhood slipped out of her wetness. When he drew back, he looked into her eyes. "Tonight was great."

"Tonight *was* great. I really enjoyed it. And this. And you."

Should I? he asked himself. *Oh, what the hell.* "And you too. I love you, babe."

She grinned. "I love you too. I'm so happy we found each other."

You may not be in a couple of days, Landon's brain hummed. He'd met her parents. Now it was time she met his.

And he had a feeling it wasn't going to go quite as well.

* * *

"Six thirty. Don't be late."

"Yes, ma'am. I won't be. Bye." It had taken some cajoling, but his mother had agreed to dinner the following evening at his parents' house. He wondered if she'd cook, or if she'd have the housekeeper do it, but he knew the answer already. His next chore would be to break the news to Jerrica.

God have mercy on his soul.

* * *

"Do I look okay?" She fretted with the hem of her little dress and then checked to make sure she hadn't lost an earring.

"Babe, you look adorable. And I like the whatever-you-call-them under the dress."

"My leggings?"

"Yeah. Those. The dress is a little short, so wearing those means my mom won't have a fit when I talk to her later."

Jerrica rolled her eyes. This was a mistake, a huge

mistake. They weren't going to like her, not one bit. She could already tell Landon was thinking that, even if he would never say it. There was nothing she could do about it, though. She was just who she was, and they'd have to deal with it. Hopefully, Landon could too.

A long, sweeping driveway led back through the trees and when they came out on the other side, a huge house stood in the middle of an enormous green space, its columns white and pristine. "Wow. This is some house. Did you grow up here?"

"No. We lived in Riverdale Estates when I was growing up. They built this house about fifteen years ago. Come on." Taking his hand, she let him lead her to the front door and open it. "Mom? Dad? We're here."

A tall, statuesque woman appeared in the foyer, and Jerrica had to stifle a gasp. She looked for all the world like Bea Arthur dressed for her part as Dorothy on *The Golden Girls*. "Hello, son. And who do we have here?"

"This is my friend, Jerrica. Babe, this is my mother, Louella Fox."

"Pleasure to meet you," Jerrica managed to choke out as she extended a hand. Maybe she wasn't supposed to do that. Perhaps she was supposed to curtsy. She wasn't sure.

Louella's hand closed around hers tightly. "And a pleasure to meet you. My, you're a tiny little thing! And so ... cute. Landon, your father's out on the patio. You're welcome to go out and introduce our guest."

"Thanks, Mom." Once again, he took her hand and Jerrica let him lead her through the house. Their living room was the size of her parents' entire home, or very close to it.

Jerrica could see Dr. Fox the elder sitting out on the patio, a cigar in his hand and some kind of magazine in his lap. When they stepped out the door, Landon called out, "Dad! I'd like you to meet my friend, Jerrica. Babe, this is my dad, Robert."

"Pleasure to meet you, my dear!" the older man said, and Jerrica could tell he meant it. He was warm and had a pleasant smile. "Glad you could come and join us tonight. Landon hasn't told us a thing about you. I suppose he was planning to surprise us! Say, you look familiar to me. Do I know you from somewhere? Perhaps where you work …"

"Yes, sir. I'm an ER nurse at Community General."

"That's where I've seen you! Yes, Jerrica! I remember that name. I thought it was most unusual and very pretty. Have a seat, have a seat! I'll put this thing out if it's bothering you," he said and motioned with the cigar.

"Oh, no, sir. It's not bothering me. Please. Don't put it out on my account," Jerrica assured him.

Landon looked around. "Where's Liella?"

Robert's eyes closed and he sighed. "Your mother told her we were having a guest for dinner and we haven't seen her since. I'm guessing she's holed up in that room up there, hiding out. It's not like you were bringing a football team to meet us, just one woman, and a small one at that!" Robert said and winked.

"I'll go up and talk to her if you'll entertain Jerrica for a minute or two," Landon said, standing. Jerrica felt a moment of panic as she realized she'd be left with his father. "Be right back." He was gone before she could protest.

"Ahhh, Landon. He's quite a fellow, that one. Did he tell you he played football in high school?"

"No, sir, but that doesn't surprise me."

"He did, and he was very good. He could've gone to school on football alone. Very smart. I.Q. in the high one fifties. I guess that's why we find it so hard to accept his choice of vocation."

Well, shit. Here we go, Jerrica thought as she flipped through the index cards in her head, trying to come up with something to say that would defend Landon without being inflammatory. "He works really hard and he loves what he does. He's making a difference in the community. I have a lot of respect for that."

"Brandon and I make a difference in the community, and we don't do it running into burning buildings. I hear he lost a friend not too long ago in a fire."

"Yes, sir, but it was from a head injury, not the fire itself. Besides, they don't just run into burning buildings. It's very carefully choreographed from outside, and they take all kinds of precautions."

"At any rate, it's a dangerous profession. His mother and I—"

"Here you are! Maria, they're out here! Well, well, well—who do we have here? Brandon Fox. And you are?"

"Jerrica Ligon. We've met. I'm an ER nurse over at Community General."

The expression on Brandon's face turned from gleeful to sour. "I remember you. Signed him out and took him home with you."

"Signed him out?" Robert asked. "What's this about?"

"Your eldest son was injured during a fire that killed his friend. Isn't that correct, Miss Ligon?"

"Yes, but—"

"And he not only had a deep scalp lac but a concussion as well, isn't that correct?"

"Yes, but—"

"He was going to leave AMA and go back to the fire, am I right?"

From somewhere behind her, she heard Landon mutter, "Holy fuck. Just what I need. What the hell are *you* doing here?"

"Boys, let's calm down and try to get along, shall we?" Jerrica heard Louella say. When she turned, she got a big surprise.

Standing beside Landon was a woman, and she was probably six feet tall. That wasn't the surprise. What shocked Jerrica was her shape. She was without a doubt the skinniest person Jerrica had ever seen alive. She looked like a walking corpse, her bones and joints all protruding and her cheeks sunken in. There was a darkness about her eyes that was positively terrifying.

Her thoughts were interrupted by Landon's voice. "Oh, I'm trying to get along, but I come out here to find him grilling Jerrica about me."

"You didn't tell them you'd been hurt?" Brandon asked shrilly.

"No, because it wasn't a big deal!" Landon fired back, then turned to Jerrica. "He has no right to treat you that way." Turning back to Brandon, he lashed out. "How would you feel if I did Maria that way, cornered her and quizzed her about you? You wouldn't like that either. You got a question about me, you ask *me*. Got that?"

"Like you'd tell the truth," Brandon mumbled.

Landon's eyes flashed with fire. "Oh, now I'm a liar?"

"Boys!" Louella's bellowing voice cut through it all. "Enough! This is no way to behave in front of a guest! Jerrica, my dear, I don't think you've met Liella. Liella, this is Jerrica, Landon's friend."

The woman bobbled from side to side oddly before she said, "Hi. Liella. Nice to meet you."

"It's nice to meet you too. Landon's told me so much about all of you."

Those dark eyes almost bugged out. "What has he told you about me? Landon, what have you said about me?" She dropped her voice and hissed, "Does she know?"

"Calm down, sis. Jerrica's not one to judge anybody. She'd really like to get to know you, wouldn't you, babe?"

"I would." Jerrica inched closer until she could reach out a hand to Liella. "I'd love to get to know you. Maybe after dinner we could sit and chat."

The young woman never took Jerrica's hand, and she felt awkward standing there "Maybe. I dunno. Can I go back upstairs now?" Liella asked.

"No. We're getting ready to eat. Dinner's on the table, so could we all please move to the dining room?" It sounded like a question, but coming from Louella, it was really more of an order.

Jerrica wound up sitting right across from Brandon. Maria sat across from Landon, and Liella sat on his right, with his dad at the end and Louella at the other end. The food was amazing, and they all managed to be cordial. "Maria, dear, that's a stunning ensemble you're wearing. Where did you get it?" Louella asked her daughter-in-law.

"I drove to Cincinnati. I wish we had a Nordstrom in Louisville, but all we have is a Nordstrom Rack, and that's just not going to do at all," the younger woman whined.

"Of course not. If only we had a Neiman Marcus but, of course, that will never happen," Louella said with a sigh. "So where do you shop, dear?" Louella directed toward Jerrica. Out of the blue, she felt

Landon squeeze her thigh and she felt better immediately.

"Mostly Target and Walmart. I like Meijer too. I buy a lot of things there." Without looking up at the two women, she took a bite of lima beans and chewed thoughtfully. No one said a word.

"Well, isn't this a good steak?" Landon asked, trying to get the conversation started again, but Jerrica was miserable.

"It's very good," she answered. "Everything is very good. And I love your dishes, Mrs. Fox."

"Thank you. They've been passed down through the family from one of my great-grandmothers on my mother's side. Cabbage rose, I believe that pattern is called."

"They're very pretty, and I like the plates under them too," she said, knowing she sounded stupid.

"Chargers. They're called chargers. Thank you. I like to use them when we're having more formal dinners."

She could feel herself tanking. There was little to talk about, and she was bombing at everything she tried. To her shock, the next voice she heard was Liella's. "Jerrica, do you like fish?"

"You mean going fishing?"

"No. I mean, like tropical fish? I have a fish tank and I really enjoy the fish."

"Oh! Yes! I like tropical fish. They're so pretty and

very, very interesting. Do yours come to the top to be fed?"

"Yes! They're really smart. I'd love to show them to you later if you'd like to see them."

"Yes, very much." Jerrica wanted to cry. The one person in the family who was the most awkward and the most damaged had come to her aid. Liella would never understand how grateful she was for that little bit of help.

The conversation around the table was sparse and stilted until everyone was finished eating, and they all retired to the great room. Jerrica felt a little ill there. Around the room were stuffed carcasses of dozens of kinds of animals, and it was obvious the elder Dr. Fox liked to hunt. She found the whole thing creepy. They'd no more than sat down when Liella said, "Oh, Jerrica! Let's go look at my fish."

"Sure! I'd love to." She followed the tall, dark woman up the stairs and down the hallway until they came to a door at the end of the hall. Liella opened it and swept her arm inward.

It looked like a ten-year-old girl's room, with pink walls and plush animals everywhere. Against one wall sat an enormous fish tank. "Oh, my. It's huge!"

"Yeah. I love it. It's so peaceful. I like to watch them swim around and do their little fishy things. I have all the stuff to take care of them, and I like to turn out the lights and watch them with their light on."

"I can see how they'd be very peaceful."

"Yeah. They really calm me down." Without looking at her, Liella asked, "Jerrica, can I talk to you, girl to girl?"

"Of course."

The woman nodded. "Landon told you what happened to me."

"He told me how upset he's been that he couldn't help you."

"He couldn't have helped me if he'd been there. It all happened so fast. But I just wanted to know, what do you think I might be able to do to be normal again?"

"Oh, honey, I don't know you well enough to be able to say, but I do know this. Normal is highly over-rated because nobody really knows what it is. What's normal for one person isn't for another. So saying you want to be normal? You're normal for you. Do you see a therapist?"

"I used to, but it didn't do any good," she said, her head bowed. "It's hopeless."

"It's not hopeless. Listen, I heard of a new therapy. Let me see if I can find the information and I'll give it to you. It's for PTSD, and they say it really works."

"That's what I have. PTSD. It's horrible. Nobody knows …"

Jerrica reached out a hand and without saying a word, Liella took it. "You want to get better. That means you will. And if you need somebody to talk to, you can call me anytime. I mean it. I'll be glad to sit and talk to you unless I'm at work. And if I'm there, I'll call you back, I promise."

Those big dark eyes got even bigger. "You'd do that for me?"

"Sure. You're Landon's sister, and I love Landon, so I love you."

"I don't have girlfriends. Maybe we can be girl-friends."

"Of course! That would be fun! Now, I'd better get back downstairs before Landon wonders what's happened to me, but I meant what I said." Rising from where she'd knelt in front of the fish tank, Jerrica spied a pad of paper and pencil on the dresser. She strode to it and wrote her phone number down. "There. That's my number. Leave me a message so I know it's you and I'll call you back. After that, I'll have your number. Does that sound good?"

"That sounds wonderful. Thanks, Jerrica. I'm going to stay up here for a while. If I don't see you again before you leave, it was good to meet you and I'm happy to make a new friend."

"Same here, honey. Hang in there." As she closed the door behind her, she smiled. Liella wasn't nearly as fragile as Landon thought she was—she just needed some encouragement from someone outside the family. God knew they weren't big on that.

Landon looked none too happy when she got back downstairs, and she sensed that he, his parents, and his brother had been arguing. Instead of sitting, she said, "Hey, babe, work tomorrow and I've gotta—"

"Yeah, we should be going." It took less than a second for him to leap to his feet, and she realized she'd done a good job of giving him a way out. "Mom, Dad, thanks for dinner."

"Yes, Dr. and Mrs. Fox, thank you for having me over. The food was delicious, and I enjoyed meeting all of you. You too, Brandon and Maria."

"Nice meeting you," Brandon returned, but Maria just nodded. It didn't matter—Landon was already dragging her toward the front door.

They were out on the main road before she finally heard Landon let out the breath he'd been holding all evening. "Holy shit, that was worse than I expected," he muttered.

"Did you get a chance to tell them about the ceremony?"

"Yeah. My dad said, 'And we'd want to celebrate you moving up the ladder toward your death *why*?' It took everything I had in me to not roll my eyes."

"So they're not coming?"

"I have no idea. I'm going to send them invitations anyway. Brandon and Maria too. I extend the olive branch; it's up to them to reach out and take it. If they don't, they don't. I can't make them do it, and I'm not going to waste time and energy worrying about it."

"Nordstrom and Nieman Marcus," Jerrica muttered under her breath.

"What?"

"Nothing. Nothing at all. So we got that over with. Now what?"

"Now we go home and act like nothing happened," Landon said with a little grin. "Our lives go on, babe."

They were within a mile of her duplex when she saw something up ahead. "What's that?"

"Looks like an ambulance or a truck." As he answered her, she could see more lights behind it. "What the hell? See that knob on the left? Turn that on," he instructed, pointing to a radio mounted below his dash.

When she turned the knob, the radio came to life. "Station Three, this is central dispatch. Respond to structure fire, one oh seven East Main Street. Repeat, respond to structure fire, one oh seven East Main Street. Copy?"

"Copy that, central dispatch."

"Station Four, Station Four, central dispatch. Respond to structure fire, one oh seven East Main Street. Report to Captain Martin from Station Two on arrival. Copy?"

"Copy that, central dispatch," another voice answered.

Landon skidded into a parking lot and wheeled the truck around just in time to see two aerial trucks and a pumper/tanker truck roar by. "What are you doing?" Jerrica asked.

"I've got to at least go see what's going on. That's

across the street from the big one the other night." As he drove, she watched him put down the truck's window, fish a light from under the seat, and slap it onto the cab's roof. "I can't believe this. Another one. At this rate, there won't be anything left of downtown pretty soon."

On their arrival it was no surprise to find the whole building engulfed in flames. They shot thirty feet into the air above the twenty-five-foot structure, and there were firefighters everywhere. "You can't do anything, babe. You don't have your turnout gear."

"I know, and I feel so fucking helpless." Jerrica took in his face as he watched his coworkers and friends scurrying around, manhandling hoses and working with the trucks. Two bucket trucks had shown up and water was being poured into the inferno from above. Through it all, she could tell Landon was assessing everything he was seeing, visually measuring things like the perimeter and how far a wall could fall, and generally torturing himself as he sat there, unable to do anything.

After twenty minutes, she laid a hand softly on his arm. "Babe, let's go. There's nothing you can do. They've got it under control, I can tell. Come on."

"But I—"

"No, Landon. Let's just go." He reluctantly started the truck, pulled the light off the roof, and headed back toward her place.

Jerrica watched his face as he drove. That man she

loved, he was brave and fearless. If he was that brave and fearless over a simple fire, a thing he hated, how brave and fearless would he be in protecting her, the woman he loved?

And she knew she'd never have anything to fear again.

* * *

"They'll be here in a few minutes!" Jerrica was beyond excited. She hadn't seen Elizabeth in years, and she also knew her cousin had, until recently, been unable to leave her apartment for any length of time. Now she was with a new guy, Cade, and he'd been able to help her a lot. On top of that, he was a firefighter too, and she was sure he and Landon would have a lot to talk about. They'd wanted to come and visit, so instead of just making it a regular visit, Jerrica had Landon send them an invitation to his promotion ceremony, and Elizabeth had been excited to come.

The couple who stepped through the gate looked a little travel weary. "Oh, god, it's so good to see you!" Jerrica screamed and ran to hug Elizabeth.

"Good to see you too, cuz," Beth said, but she slurred her words a little.

Jerrica stepped back and looked into her face. She seemed kind of drowsy. "Are you okay?"

"Xanax." In confusion, Jerrica turned to the tall man standing beside her cousin. "Hi. Cade." As he shook her hand, he explained. “She has to have it to fly. She’ll be okay in a couple of hours. We just need to get to your place and let her rest.”

“Oh, okay. I’m Jerrica. This is my boyfriend, Landon.”

“Good to meet you,” Landon said as he took Cade’s hand. “Let’s get her to the house.”

Once Beth was settled on the bed in the guest bedroom, Jerrica rejoined the guys in the living room. “So you’re being promoted to lieutenant?” Cade asked from inside his cup of hot, steaming coffee.

“Yeah. I never thought I’d make it.” Landon set his mug down. “So you’re with San Antonio?”

“Yeah, Station Two.”

“Mine is Station Two here! Isn’t that a coincidence? So, has anything exciting been happening around your house’s district?”

“We’ve had a few small dwelling fires but, thank god, nothing big lately. I hear you guys have had a string of really big fires.”

“We have. All in our downtown area.”

“And what’s causing them?”

Landon shrugged. “I have no idea. Haven’t heard from the fire inspector yet either. My captain called and asked, but they said the reports aren’t in yet.”

“How long ago was the first one?”

“About two months ago.”

Cade snorted. “Somebody needs to lean on that guy. You guys need to find out what’s going on down there.”

"Boy, do I ever agree with that. One of my buddies was killed in the same fire where I was injured. I'm not too happy with this no-answer bullshit."

"So these were all in your downtown area?"

"Yeah. At this rate, there won't *be* a downtown area pretty soon." As soon as the words slipped from Landon's mouth, Jerrica saw Cade's eyebrows shoot up.

"You're thinking something. What is it?" Jerrica asked.

"I'm just thinking that there may be a pattern if they're all in the same area. You should draw yourself a little handmade map, map them out, see where the next one is. Hopefully, there won't be a next one, but if there is, that could be telling."

Landon nodded. "You've got a point. I never thought about that. I'll do it and see what I come up with."

"Of course, if there is a pattern, you'll have to figure out what it means. That'll be the hard part."

"Are you guys talking shop?" a feminine voice asked from the hallway and Beth appeared in the entrance.

"Of course. They can't help themselves!" Jerrica answered, laughing.

But for the rest of the afternoon, something about the conversation bothered Jerrica. What if there *was* a pattern? What if someone *was* trying to burn all the buildings down? What would that mean?

And how would they ever find out?

CHAPTER 6

They were all there. Robert, Louella, Brandon, Maria, and Liella, although she seemed terrified. Jerrica's mom, her dad, Liam, and Darlene. Of course, Beth and Cade were there. All the guys from the station who could be spared. It was quite the crowd. Jerrica had dashed about all morning, trying to get the trays of food in place, getting the special napkins she'd bought laid out in pretty patterns on the table, getting the punchbowl set up, and making sure there were enough plates for the cake and anything else anyone wanted. Captain Martin's wife, Elise, had graciously offered to come and help, and Jerrica really liked her. They'd laughed and talked the entire time, and she felt comfortable around Elise. Beth had helped too, and she was thankful for the two of them.

Then it was time for the ceremony. Landon had

refused to let her come in before he was dressed, and when he finally let her step in, he took her breath away. "Oh my god, you look so handsome in your dress uniform!" she exclaimed.

"Thank you. I don't get to wear it very often. You were at work during the funeral or you would've seen it then." He straightened his tie and looked in the mirror as Jerrica watched, her heart swelling with pride. She couldn't imagine how she'd feel when he was awarded his new badge—her heart would probably burst!

The ceremony wasn't long. Captain Martin spoke first and talked about Landon's career with the department, where he'd served, and the kind of work ethic he exhibited. Then the battalion chief, Chief Murphy, talked about the life of a firefighter and how hard the work was. To Jerrica's surprise, the deputy chief was a woman, and she rose and spoke to the families about how to support the firefighters in their family. She hoped Landon's parents and brother were listening during that part. Surely it would make them a little more cooperative and supportive. But maybe not.

Then it was the big moment. She assumed the man was the big chief. His name was Doug Roberts, and he stood and walked to the podium. "At this time, I'd like to ask Captain Martin to join me." Captain Martin rose and stood beside Chief Roberts, and in his hand he held a small, blue velvet box. "Firefighter one eight three nine five, would you stand please and join us on the podium?" With just a brief squeeze of Jerrica's hand, Landon rose and made his way to the podium. As Chief Roberts spoke, Captain Martin took Landon's hat. He took the emblem from the front of it and put a new one on, sort of like a big pin. Jerrica couldn't see what it said, but she assumed it said *lieutenant*. Then he put some kind of patch at the top of both sleeves of the jacket, then added a cord through one epaulet. When he was finished, he handed Landon something that looked like a wallet and shook Landon's hand. "A grateful community wants to reward your diligence, your determination, your dedication, and your decision to be a civil servant of the highest order, risking your life for your family and neighbors," Chief Roberts said. Jerrica knew it was over when he said, "Please join me in welcoming the newest member of the Taylorsville Fire and Rescue Department, *Lieutenant* Landon Simpson Fox."

In seconds, everyone was on their feet, cheering, especially the guys from the house. Landon turned to face the crowd and opened the small, wallet-like object. Inside it was a brand-new shield, his number emblazoned on it and the word *Lieutenant* engraved above the crest. The room was full of family and friends, but he looked directly at her, and she gave him the biggest smile she could muster as tears coursed down her cheeks. Damn, she was proud of him! Until he'd met her, he'd had no family to support him or help him, but that was over as long as she was around. He had her, and she'd always be there for him.

"Please join us for refreshments at the table in the other room, and thanks to everyone for coming," Chief Roberts said, but as everyone walked away, she noticed Landon stayed. In a minute, she saw why—the local paper was there to take pictures, and she knew they would show up in the edition for the next morning. How great would that be?

She was busy putting out more napkins when she felt a familiar presence behind her. When his arms wrapped around her waist, she smiled. "Thank you for being here for me and for all this," he whispered into her right ear. "It means everything to me to have you with me."

"And it means everything to me to be here for you. And I'll always be here for you," she said and pulled one of his hands to her lips to kiss his knuckles. "Now get down there and cut your cake! Everybody wants a piece and nobody wants to cut it!"

"Yes, ma'am!" he said with a laugh and gave her a little salute. She watched as Beth, Stingray, and Betsy shot pictures of him cutting it with their phones, and she was sure they'd share them with her later. A pain shot through her chest as she watched Robert, Louella, Liella, Brandon, and Maria huddle in one corner of the back of the room, appearing to want to be anywhere but there. Couldn't they at least congratulate their son and brother and wish him well? The rest of the community certainly seemed to be able to.

She was cleaning up in the civic center's kitchen when Beth stepped in, her hand in Cade's. "Where did Landon's parents go?"

"I dunno. Did they leave?"

"Looks like they did. Did they even speak to him?"

Jerrica shook her head. "Probably not."

"Why?"

"They hate that he's a firefighter. They wanted him to be a doctor like his dad and brother." Talking about it almost brought Jerrica to tears. She knew they were afraid for his safety, but if she could tolerate it, they should be able to.

"That's horrible. Well, Uncle Jeff and Aunt Amy are out there bending his ear, and your mom's hugged him twice already. I suppose he has parents now, huh?"

Jerrica straightened and sniffled. "Yes. Yes, he does. He has my family now. If they want nothing to do with him, the Ligons will stand by him."

Beth nodded, smiled, and patted her and Cade's clasped hands. "Yes they will. He'll always be able to count on all of you."

He would. Jerrica would see to that.

His uniform was hanging in the back, his shoes, belt, and tie in the seat. They stopped on the way home and got milkshakes, then sat in the parking lot and drank them. They'd almost finished them when she finally asked, "Did your parents even speak to you today?"

"My dad just said, "Congratulations, son, if this is really what you want to do.' Then he walked away. Mom, Brandon, and Maria never spoke to me. They barely looked at me. Liella was too terrified to come out of the corner." There was a sadness in his eyes that Jerrica couldn't miss, and it cut her to the bone.

"Beth said my mom nearly worried you to death hugging you," she said, trying to lighten the mood a little.

He chuckled. "Yeah, I think Amy is going to be one of my biggest fans. She told me over and over how glad they were to be there and how proud she was of me. Not the same, but … it's something, and I'm grateful for their support."

"You have family now. You can always go to my parents and ask for help or support. They'll always be there for you," Jerrica told him as she took his hand.

"That's what your dad told me, and I don't think your dad has the ability to bullshit anybody. He doesn't seem the type."

That made Jerrica laugh. "No, he's no good at bull-shitting, that's for sure! He's the worst liar I ever met!"

They both quieted for a few seconds before Landon whispered, "I did it. I'm a lieutenant."

Jerrica laughed and gave him a wink. "Someday you'll be the fire chief. You'll take Chief Roberts' job. I'm sure of it!"

He leaned back against the truck's door and grinned. "I don't care as long as I have you."

She smiled her sweetest smile at him. "Then I guess you'll never care at all."

* * *

Cade and Beth had gone to dinner with Liam and Darlene so the two cousins could catch up, and that left Landon and Jerrica home alone. When she stepped into the den, she found Landon sitting in his favorite recliner with a legal pad and pencil. "Whatcha doin'?"

"What Cade suggested. And look at this, babe." He put the footrest down and sat up, so Jerrica sat on the arm of the chair and peered down at the pad. "These are the buildings that burned. And look at this." He drew a bigger square around everything. "They all fall within these four blocks."

"Are all the other buildings in those areas empty?"

"Not all of them, but most of them. This one here," he said, pointing to a rectangle, "is—"

"St. Xavier's Church," Jerrica interrupted.

"Yes. And this one is a daycare. This one right here," he said, pointing to another one, "is a branch of the public library. Unfortunately, I think the other buildings are empty."

"So how many empty buildings are there?"

"Three more."

"And if one of them burns?"

"I'm going to the sheriff. Something's not right with this picture." Landon laid the pad on the coffee table to his left and sat there, his fingers steepled and touching his lower lip. "I think Cade's onto something, and I think this might be big. But we won't know for sure unless another one of those buildings burns. But what if the fire inspector and fire marshal are in on this? They still haven't ruled on the cause of the earlier fires."

"I think you'd need to talk to Captain Martin before you speak to the sheriff. He might not be happy about you going over his head," she warned.

"You may be right. But I'm really worried. If this is deliberate and there's a reason, what about the three buildings that are occupied? Little kids. Old people. Students. Homemakers. All kinds of people frequent those three places. Will some of them get hurt? Whoever is doing this … do they even care?"

"Probably not or they wouldn't be doing it to start with. Face it, there's been another fire since Carlos died. If they didn't care that a firefighter was killed, they wouldn't care about little kids or old people."

"You're right. I don't know what to do, but I have to do *something*."

"Just keep your ear to the ground. That's all you can do. You have no proof of anything right now." Jerrica was interrupted by the sound of the front door.

"Anybody home?" she heard Beth call out.

"We're back here. Cade, I think you and Landon need to talk."

She and Beth retreated to the kitchen while Cade and Landon discussed his theories. Jerrica wasn't sure she wanted to know what they came up with.

The possibilities were too terrifying.

* * *

The sky was blue, the sun was bright, and a bird was singing on the power line directly above her parking spot when Jerrica headed into the hospital a couple of weeks later. It was a beautiful day, the kind of day she wanted to play hooky on. She could think of a million things she'd like to do outdoors, not the least of which was finding some nice hanging baskets for Landon's front porch. In reality, she'd actually started thinking of it as her front porch too, especially since he'd told her to just move in the week before. She hadn't had to think one single second before she'd agreed to it.

But inside, it was an odd kind of day. The emergency room was extremely quiet, so much so that they let three of the nurses go upstairs to different floors to work. One patient came in with a heart attack, but Mina caught that one, and pretty soon he was being whisked off for a catheterization anyway. "Taking my break outside," Jerrica called to Mallory.

"Don't get a sunburn!" the girl called back.

Sitting on a concrete bench out by the ambulance

bay, Jerrica leaned back on the heels of her hands and lifted her face to the sun, letting the rays warm her skin. She thought about Landon. He was working that morning, would work until four that afternoon, and she was planning to fix a big pot roast for dinner. Boy, he'd love that! Sitting there in the brightness, she fantasized about watching him peel the carrots and potatoes, those strong biceps flexing as he ran the peeler over the vegetables. She was almost ready to go back inside when she heard something that sounded like thunder. Her eyes scanned the sky, but there wasn't a cloud anywhere. Curious, she hopped up and made her way back inside.

It took about two seconds for her to figure out what she'd heard. The radio at the central desk was going crazy with all kinds of transmissions. "What's happened?"

"Explosion downtown. Another building fully engulfed. I don't know what's going on, but they're calling out units from everywhere," Mallory reported.

Jerrica's heart began to race and her mouth went dry. Was Landon being called out? She could hear the transmissions, and sure enough, they called for Station Two. His house was going out, and all she could do was stand there and wait.

She paced the hallway outside the cubicles. *Please, please, please, don't let any of the guys get hurt,* she heard a voice whispering inside her head. She knew them all, had met them all, and they weren't just faceless responders to her, not anymore. They were friends and Landon's coworkers. Fear had almost taken her down when she heard Mallory yell, "Jerrica? We've got a patient out here!"

Two men stood there. Both had on turnout coats, and one of them was bent almost double. "Can I help you?"

"Yes, ma'am. He needs some help. He has burns on his arms."

"Come on! What happened?" she asked as she ran to the nearest cubicle, the men following her.

"We're all down there fighting the fires and he got a little too close. Show her." The second man pulled off his coat and, sure enough, his forearms were badly burned.

"How did you get here?"

"Uh, we took a cab. There was one nearby and that was faster than waiting for an ambulance." That struck Jerrica as odd. She'd never heard Landon refer to an ambulance as anything but a bus.

"I see. So let's get some vitals on you and—"

"Oh, god, it hurts! Can't you do something to help the pain?"

"Let me get a doctor to—"

"Please! I can't stand it!"

Jerrica grabbed a pot of ointment from the cabinet. "Here. Let's put some of this on it. It can't hurt it, and it may make it feel better until we can get it evaluated." She smeared the clear ointment on thick. "Better?"

"A little."

"Good. Let me get the doctor and some forms for you to fill out." As she ran out, she passed the desk. "Call Dr. Fielding and get him down here. This man's burns are bad."

"Sure thing." The page went out and Jerrica knew all they could do was wait. She didn't have the authority to treat the man, and she felt horrible that a firefighter had to suffer just to wait on a doctor.

But when she made her way back to the cubicle, she overheard the conversation between the two men, and she stopped.

"Do you think she realizes we're fakes?"

"Probably not. I thought the story sounded good enough."

"Oh, god, this hurts! I hope they get back here soon!"

"If we get any indication they're onto us, we'll have to leave."

"I can't leave! My arms are burned too badly! I could die from this!"

"You won't die. You'll suffer, but you won't *die*, you dumbass. Let's just admit you fucked up. The boss won't be happy about this."

"Fuck the boss. *I'm* the one who's hurt!"

Jerrica didn't know what to do. The men were obviously connected to the fire. It sounded like one of them had set it, and yet she couldn't confront them. The best she could do was let Dr. Fielding treat the man while she found some covert way to take a picture of him, contact the police, or get a message to Landon. What could she possibly do to make sure they didn't get away?

"Burn victim?" a voice behind her asked, and she turned to find Dr. Fielding standing there.

"Yes, sir. In the first cubicle. I put some ointment on the burns because he was complaining about the pain."

"Okay. Let's see what we've got," the physician said as he breezed in through the cubicle's curtains. "Pretty nasty burns. So you're firefighters?"

"Yes, sir. He got a little too close."

"I can see that. Hold still … That may need a graft. Let's get a derm in here pronto and see what they think. Just hang on. In the meantime, I'll have the nurse here give you a shot of Demerol to help with the pain."

"Thank you, doctor," the injured man murmured.

"Okay, here you go. I need to give this to you in your hip, if you'd like to step out," Jerrica told the other man.

"I'm fine. I'll stay right here."

She waited while the man undid his belt and his pants and pulled them down enough that she could give him the shot. As soon as she was finished, she headed out into the hallway to track down Dr. Fielding. "Sir, could I speak to you for a minute?"

"Sure, but I know what you're going to say. They're wearing athletic shoes."

"Yes, sir. And he was burned underneath his turnout coat. They're not firefighters. Look, I think—"

"Me too. I've called the police. They should be here in a couple of minutes. The whole thing looks suspicious."

"Exactly."

"Go keep them company while we wait. Start the H&P process," he said, referencing a harvesting of medical history and a physical examination.

"Yes, sir." Jerrica turned and headed toward the cubicle, dreading being in the same room with the men. She was genuinely frightened. If they were the two who'd been setting fires, what might they do if they suspected she had caught on?

She needn't have worried. When she pulled back the curtain, they were gone.

* * *

It was three thirty before the police finished questioning her, and she was embarrassed. They'd asked her to describe the men, and she couldn't really give them much. She was beating herself up for not paying attention while they were there, but there was one thing she was happy about. Not one single bus had come in while the police were there. So far, no firefighters had been injured fighting the fire, and that was something to be happy about.

When she finally got away from the hospital, she

drove downtown to see which houses were still there. Sure enough, Station Two's ladder truck was still on scene, and she could see Landon across the street, talking to two of the men who were moving barricades. She didn't mean for him to see her, but when he turned and caught her eye, he gave her a little wave, said something to the men, and jogged across the street to where she stood. "What are you doing here?" he asked.

"I just wanted to check on you. I'm headed home, and we've got to talk when you get home."

"What did I do?" he asked with a lopsided grin.

"Nothing. I saw your arsonists today."

His eyes went wide. "What? What do you mean, you saw our arsonists?"

"I'll explain later. Just finish up here and we'll talk over dinner. How much longer will you be?"

"Probably not long. Next shift will be coming on and they'll come down here to relieve us. Soon as they get here, I'll be on my way. Be careful going home. Love you."

"Love you too, babe. You be careful." She gave him a little peck and headed back to her car, then drove straight back to the house to get dinner started.

She'd just finished the roast in the pressure cooker when Landon stepped inside. "I've got to shower before I can eat," he announced. He was right. She could smell the smoke all the way back in the kitchen.

The first words out of his mouth when they sat

down at the table were, "So, tell me about this." Jerrica started the story, how the men had come in, the story they'd told about how they'd gotten there, how she and Dr. Fielding both had noticed their athletic shoes.

"So I'm convinced they're the arsonists. I overheard them talking about how mad the 'big boss' was going to be," she said, using air quotes.

"Hmmm. Well, this fire was different."

"How?"

"Whatever it was that was used to ignite it, there was natural gas trapped inside, apparently. That was the explosion. Not a lot of gas, but enough to cause a powerful combustion event."

"That would explain how he got burned when he hadn't before," Jerrica said, pondering it aloud.

"Exactly."

"And where did they get the turnout coats?"

"Could've stolen them from somewhere else miles, maybe several states, away. Doesn't happen often, but it happens. Houses have items stolen all the time. We can't watch everything every minute of the day. Sad fact, but true."

"It's Thursday night. I suppose you'll be gaming, huh?" A chuckle rumbled from Landon's throat. "Guess that's a yes. No biggie. Go get ready. I'll clean everything up. Think I'll go soak in a hot tub and read."

He kissed her forehead as he rose from the table. "Thanks, babe. I appreciate you not minding."

"You were doing it before we met. Far be it from me

to try to change you, Landon Simpson Fox!" she said, laughing.

"You're a good sport, Jerrica Karen Ligon!"

He was disappearing into the den when she yelled, "Hey, when are we going to do something about that stupid last name of mine?"

She grinned when Landon yelled back, "Anytime you want, sweetheart! Anytime you want!" It wasn't a proposal, but it wasn't half bad, she had to admit.

With the kitchen cleaned up, Jerrica ran a tub full of hot water and threw in a fizzy bath bomb. The scent of lavender filled the air, and she lit a couple of lavender-scented candles and turned off the lights. For once, she was thankful she had an ereader that had a backlit screen—she didn't need light to read by. Through the bathroom window she could see some stars and the moon, and it was a bright, clear night. Her mind wandered instead of reading, and she thought about how much they'd enjoyed Cade and Beth's visit, and how she wanted to go to San Antonio to see them sometime. The idea of getting a dog floated through her mind and she was wondering what kind they could find to adopt when her phone rang. Reaching for it, she looked at the screen: Brandy. "Hey, girl, what's up?"

"Didn't you work with Dr. Fielding today?"

"Yeah. Why?"

"He was working the afternoon. Got off at eight."

Jerrica looked at the clock. It was nine fifteen. "Yeah?"

"Somebody stabbed him in the parking lot, Jerrica. He's dead."

She sat up so abruptly that her ereader clattered to the floor. "What? Are you kidding?"

"No. One of the other doctors found him in the parking lot beside his car. Stabbed in the stomach and heart. Said even if they'd found him immediately after, it wouldn't have mattered. There was no way he could've survived."

A million things ran through Jerrica's mind but, like a spinning slot machine, two faces popped up in her thoughts. "Brandy, I've gotta go. I can't talk."

"Okay. Just thought you'd want to know."

"Yeah. Thanks. Bye." Ending the call, she dropped the phone on the floor and sat there in the tepid water.

Dr. Fielding was dead. And they'd seen her and talked to her. Oh, god, would they come after her too? Most likely. She had to talk to Landon, and then she had to get some protection. Instead of dressing, she grabbed her towel, wrapped it around her, and took off up the hallway, screaming his name.

"Babe! What's wrong!"

"Dr. Fielding is dead!" she shrieked.

"Calm down! What are you talking about?"

"Those men killed him! I'm sure of it!"

"What men? What are you—"

"The arsonists! Oh, god, they'll come after me next!" she whined, terrified.

Landon ripped the headset from his head and threw

it on the sofa. "Babe, calm down! Nobody's coming after you! You don't even know what happened for sure. How did you find out?"

"Brandy called! Oh, Landon, I just know that's who it was!"

"Okay, calm down. Let me call one of the guys I know on the force and get him to come over here, okay? I'm sure this is just a coincidence."

Jerrica ran to the bedroom and threw on her pajamas. She had to have *something* on if a police officer was coming over. In a few minutes, there was a knock at the door and Landon opened it to a Spencer County sheriff's deputy. "Blane, good to see you."

"And you too. What's going on?"

"Come on in and sit down. Want something to drink?"

The big man laughed. "What I want I can't have because I'm on duty, but I'll take coffee if you've got it!"

"Coming right up. Jerrica, this is Blane. We've known each other for years. You can talk to him."

"Yes, ma'am," the officer assured her. "Now tell me what it is you think is going on."

Jerrica told him everything she and Dr. Fielding had told the Taylorsville police officers who'd come to the hospital. When she was finished, she looked him in the eyes. "Tell me, had Dr. Fielding been robbed when he was stabbed?"

"Um, I don't think so, miss."

"It's Jerrica."

"Jerrica. Okay. But no, they distinctly said robbery didn't seem to be a motive."

"Well, see? I'm *not* crazy!" Jerrica almost yelled.

Landon patted her shoulder. "Babe, nobody said you were. Honestly, I'm concerned now. What if they *did* manage to get rid of Dr. Fielding because he could identify them? Would they come after her?"

"It's possible. Unlikely, but possible."

"And what can you offer us?" Landon asked.

"Without proof?" Blane shrugged. "Nothing."

"Great. The woman I love may be able to identify two arsonists who now may be responsible for two deaths and nobody has anything to offer us. Peachy." Landon stood and began to pace. "I obviously can't be with you every second of the day," he told Jerrica. "I don't know what to do."

"I'll be fine." But somehow, deep down, she knew she wouldn't be, and she was scared. Those guys meant business. She'd be asking people to walk her from and to her car from that point forward, and she'd be carrying a weapon too. Her daddy didn't raise her to be a victim, and she wasn't going down without a fight.

Jerrica Ligon wasn't about to let somebody rob her of her life. Not if she could do something about it.

* * *

Her supervisor worked out a plan. Jerrica called the desk when she pulled into a space in the hospital parking lot and a security officer came out and escorted her to the building. At the end of her shift, one went out with her until she was locked in her car. She didn't stop on the way to work, and she most certainly didn't stop on the way home. One day, the security guard who came out when she got to work was someone she didn't recognize, and she made him go back in and get one of the guys she *did* know before she'd get out of the car. If they didn't mind impersonating firefighters, they sure as hell would have no compunction about impersonating security guards.

Plus … the building fit. Landon drew it into the map he'd made, and it was one of the buildings within that larger space.

They'd fallen back into a regular, albeit nervous, schedule when Landon got a call he hadn't expected. "Is this Landon Fox?"

"Yes. Who's calling?"

"My name is Agent Cruz Livingston. I'm with the FBI in San Antonio. I was talking to someone you know, Cade Turner? And he asked me to call you."

"Oh! Yeah, Cade's girlfriend is related to my girlfriend. Cousins. What can I help you with?"

"It's what I can help you with. He says you're a firefighter and you've got some suspicious fires going on right now."

"We do. And a couple of deaths, although one may or may not be related."

"Why don't you start at the beginning and tell me

everything? I promise you won't bore me!" the agent said with a laugh.

Landon launched into the story, with Agent Livingston stopping him here and there to ask a question or clarify something. When he was finished, there was a long sigh from the other end of the phone. Landon was afraid to ask, but he did anyway. "Well? Do you think there's something here?"

"I absolutely do. I'm going to start doing some checking to see if this is happening in other areas. It'll be like finding a needle in a haystack, but you never know. In the meantime, start doing some checking on your end. See if you can find out if anybody has made offers on any of the properties that have burned. If they have, that might give us a clue. If you think of anything, please call me at this number anytime. Don't hesitate. Even the most seemingly insignificant thing could be important."

"Got it. Thanks. And thank you for taking the time to call me, Agent Livingston. Nobody around here can seem to help us."

"It's Cruz, and I'm not there, but I'll do what I can. Take care, and take care of Jerrica too."

"I will. Thanks." Landon listened until the phone went dead and sighed. Things were bad—really, really bad—and they'd have to get a lot worse before he and Jerrica could get any help. But he knew one thing for sure.

He'd follow up on every idea Cruz had given him

and anything else he could think of. Somewhere in everything that had happened, there had to be a clue of some kind as to what was going on. If it was there, he'd find it. He'd do anything to keep her safe.

"So he gave me some ideas, and I'm going to follow up on them," Landon told Jerrica as he described the call from Cruz while they ate dinner. "I'm going to look around too. If these guys haven't finished their work, they're around here somewhere, and face it—Taylorsville isn't that big."

"It's big enough for them to disappear into the community, babe."

Landon smiled. "I'm just trying to make you feel better."

"Know what would make me feel better?" she asked with a grin.

"No, but I know what would make *me* feel better, and I hope it's the same thing that would make *you* feel better," he said smugly.

"I have a feeling it is. So how 'bout we throw all this carryout stuff away and go make each other feel better? You're off tomorrow, right?" He nodded. "Well, so am I. That means we can stay in bed as long as we want."

He laughed aloud. "Boy, I'm liking the sound of this already!"

When he reached for her and pulled her up against him twenty minutes later between the sheets in his big bed, he blessed the heavens for sending him that woman. She was everything to him and more encouragement than he'd had in a long, long time. Everything she'd brought into his life had made it better, and there was nothing he wouldn't do for her. Their lips had barely parted when she whispered, "Landon?"

"Yeah, babe?"

"Hold me tight? I'm afraid."

He squeezed her even tighter. "There's nothing to be afraid of. I'll make sure you're okay. Nobody's going to get you on my watch."

"You can't be with me all the time."

"I wish I could, but I have to trust that you have enough sense to watch out and be careful. And I know you do."

"I wish I had half of your confidence," she mumbled.

"You're taking all the appropriate precautions. You're watching your surroundings. You're armed, and you're taking advantage of the offer of security at the hospital. All the security guards know there's a problem, and they're watching too. It seems to me that those guys weren't too bright to begin with, and I certainly don't think they're smarter than all of us. So I don't think there's anything to worry about, baby. You're mine, and I won't let anything happen to you."

She ran a finger from just under his lower lip, down his chin, then his neck, through the depression at the center of his collarbone, and straight down the center of his chest. "Do you have any idea how sexy you are when you go all alpha male on me?"

"Do you have any idea how sexy you are under me?"

Jerrica giggled. "Because you are, babe. Those are the two most beautiful tits I've ever seen, and that's the finest pussy I've ever been inside. Nobody—*nobody*—could compare to you. Ever."

"God, I love having you inside me. It's the only time I feel totally complete."

Landon grinned. "Yeah?"

"Yeah. Like everything in my world is okay."

He peppered sweet little kisses on her lips and smiled down at her again. "I love you, babe. It's ridiculous how much I love you." He stopped and gazed down into her eyes, and he made his decision that instant. "I was going to do this big fancy bullshit thing, but you know what? I don't want to. I want to do this right now." Reaching into his nightstand, he pulled out a small box. "I want you to have this, to wear it and enjoy it. I love you, and I want to marry you, make you my wife, and share my life with you, if you'll have me." He handed the little box to her and waited.

He could feel his heartbeat double as she opened it, and her eyes lit up. "Oh my god, Landon! It's beautiful!"

"Just like the woman I bought it for. Do you want it? I guess the question is, do you want me? Forever?"

"I want you for eternity. Will you slip it on my finger?"

"Sure. Here. Let's ... Oh, god, I hope it's not too tight. Ah! There we go! That looks beautiful on your finger, baby. Did I do okay?"

"You did great. Oh, I'm so excited! So how soon do

you want to do this? Or do you want to wait for a while? I mean, are we talking about we'll get married someday, or we'll get married soon, or—"

"Baby, baby. Calm down. We can get married whenever you want. I'm ready right this second, so however long it takes you to do whatever you want to do, that's fine with me as long as it's not going to be four or five years. That's just ridiculous," he said and rolled his eyes.

"No, I'm thinking let's run away somewhere and get married! Don't you think that would be fun?"

"You don't want your family there?"

She clasped her fingers behind his neck and pressed her pelvis against his. "I've always tried to figure out weddings. I think they're something that's extremely personal and intimate, and I don't understand sharing that intimate moment with five hundred people. I mean, why? What's the point? I don't get it. I'd rather it was you, me, and a couple of witnesses we found on the street. Why spend all that money and time? We get married in clothes that are comfortable, in a place we love, and do it quietly. Sweet and private."

"Future Mrs. Fox, I like the way you think," he told her and kissed her like he meant it. He pulled back and took in the sight of her, that wild tousle of blond hair, those big blue eyes, those swollen, pouty lips puffy from their kisses, and all he could think about was being buried in her warmth and softness. "I love you.

I'll marry you anywhere, anytime. Doesn't matter, as long as you're my wife."

"Doesn't matter to me, as long as you're my husband." She kissed him back and bit his lower lip. "You're everything I could ever want and all I'll ever need, babe."

"You're on the pill, right?"

"Yep."

"No more condoms?"

She smiled. "No more condoms."

"Thank you, Jesus!" Landon yelled and rolled until she was under him, both of them laughing the whole time. "Now, I suppose it's time I claim you."

"Do it. Claim me. I want to be yours."

"Ready for something a little different?"

The smile she gave him was pure seduction. "What do you have in mind?"

Landon reached into his nightstand and took out a little drawstring bag. From it he pulled two items, and his hard cock hardened further as he took in the sight of her watching him attach the nipple clamps to her hardened buds. They had blue jewels on them, and he'd bought them because they sparkled like her eyes. She gasped as they bit in, and he whispered, "A little more." One turn of the thumbscrew on each one and she gasped again. He had her right where he wanted her.

Sliding until he was between her legs, he lifted her thighs, dropped them over his shoulders, and buried his face in her slit just to listen to her howl. She was wet, so wet, and he couldn't get enough of her sweetness and saltiness. When he ran his tongue inside her, she cried out, and when he dragged it up her slit and circled her tiny little pearl, she groaned. Ah, the groaning—he loved the groaning. "Get ready, girl. I plan to make you come apart."

He gripped her thighs as he pressed them into his shoulders and she wiggled and squirmed, trying to get away from his tongue, but he wasn't having any of that. Nope, she'd take it and love it, regardless the noise she was making. Three minutes in and she was mumbling and making no sense, and he was determined to wring more out of her. Driving her crazy was all he had on his mind, and he seemed to be doing a good job of it. Her back arched until nothing but her head and shoulders were on the bed and she fought to pump her hips, but Landon held her legs tightly and wouldn't let go. He wouldn't stop either, and pretty soon she was nearing another orgasm, one he knew would be stronger and more violent than the first one. "Oh, god, please, baby, I don't think I can take it," she moaned.

He wanted to tell her, *I'm not giving you a choice,* but he couldn't. His mouth was occupied and being used for something far better than talking. He let his tongue circle the tiny, hard little nub, then sucked it in between his lips before lapping at it again. A quick look told him her hands were gripping the headboard of the bed until her knuckles were white, and he almost laughed. This would be spectacular, he knew, if he could just get her to turn loose. As she struggled, the jewels on the clamps glittered in the light, and Landon didn't think he'd ever seen anything as beautiful as that woman in that moment, straining against him, fighting that orgasm with everything she had. He'd let it go on long enough, and he planned to end it right then.

Slipping his tongue under the hood of her little nub, he found the upper left quadrant and began to run his tongue back and forth over it there in the crease. And that got the reaction he was looking for. "Oh, Landon. Oh, Landon, no. Please, no. Landon, please, no, no, no. Oh, god, Landon, oh, please, please, oh, oh ... OHHHH-HHHH!" With her body rigid, it was all he could do to hold onto her thighs, but he didn't stop, didn't even slow down, and he could tell she was growing frantic. "Landon! Oh, shit, babe! Stop! Please, stop! Oh, I can't take any more! Please, babe, please! Stop! Please? Stop!"

And there it was—begging. That's what he'd wanted her to do, beg him to stop, and she had. Rising up on his knees, he pressed her thighs upward and slammed himself into her. Her white-knuckled clutching of the headboard continued as she cried out, "Oh, yeah, baby, fuck me!"

"You want a fucking, a fucking's what you're gonna get, little girl. I'm gonna fuck you until you can't walk." He pounded her, making sure she was curled up until his cock head was hitting that sweet spot inside her, and he listened with satisfaction as she groaned out another orgasm, her sheath pulsing around him. Jesus, she was so hot and tight and wet! It was building again, and he reached up and yanked the nipple clamps to drive her over the edge again. All she had for that was a low, guttural moan that went on and on as he used her body relentlessly. She wanted to be claimed? Well, by god, that was what he was doing, and she'd be his when he was finished with her. He'd never have to worry about anyone else—no one else would ever be able to satisfy her the way he did.

Too soon he felt his balls draw up against his body and he knew his own climax was imminent. God, he'd wanted it to last so much longer! "No condom, baby. You're going to feel it when I come. Do you want it?"

"I want it so bad, babe. So bad. Please. I need it," she begged in a voice hoarse with longing.

"Then … you'll … get … it, aww yeah," he mumbled as he shot his essence inside her. Three more small strokes and he was spent.

Landon fell on his back beside her and lay there, out of breath and almost wheezing. "Oh, god, baby, that was some kind of awesome." He waited a few seconds before he said, "Jerrica? Babe, you okay?"

"I'm not sure I can move."

Landon laughed. "Well, you wanted me to claim you! I guess you've been claimed, huh?"

"Holy hell, I won't be able to walk for three days!" she moaned.

"I really worked you over, didn't I?"

"Yeah, you did. And where did you get these?" she

asked, toying with the jewels on the clamps. "They're really pretty."

"At the adult store."

"Are you trying to corrupt me, Mr. Fox?"

"I dunno. Is it working?"

"Maybe."

Landon laughed. "I'll eventually get you the way I want you. I've just gotta teach you. We should go sometime. To the adult store, I mean."

"I'd like that. Can I get a vibrator?"

"You have me. Do you need one?"

"For when you're gone in the evenings maybe?"

"So maybe I can use it on you?" he asked, wiggling his eyebrows and making her laugh.

"Maybe! Now, take these clamps off so I can snuggle with you," she said. She winced as he pinched them open and removed them. "Ah, better."

"But did they help?"

"Hell yeah. I've *never* had an orgasm like that before! It was awesome! I'd say let's do it again, but I think it might kill me."

Landon wrapped his arms around her and pulled her into him again. "We've got all night and part of tomorrow. Let's get some sleep and we can start again in a couple of hours if you want."

"Oh, I want, big boy. Trust me, I want. And babe?"

"Yeah?"

"Your cum inside me? I've wanted that for so long. I'm glad we're where we are in this relationship, that we're moving in this direction. I want eternity with you, Landon, and it still won't be long enough."

He kissed her forehead. "Eternity with you won't be long enough for me either. I love you, baby."

"I love you too. Now and forever."

Now and forever. Those words echoed in his ears as he nodded off and dreamed of a tall, white cake, his big bed, and a little girl with eyes like Jerrica's.

CHAPTER 7

Where were those damn potatoes? Jerrica looked high and low, but she couldn't figure out what Landon did with them. They'd been first on the list when she asked him to stop at the store the evening before. Going shopping was out of the question for her as long as the arsonists were still running around loose, but it sucked not being able to buy groceries herself. She finally gave up and called him. He answered with a cheery, "Hello, baby!"

"Landon, where are the potatoes?"

There was silence for a few seconds before he asked, "Is this a trick question?"

"No. It's a simple question. Where are the potatoes?"

"What potatoes?"

"The ones I asked you to bring home yesterday."

It was silent again until he finally said, "Was I supposed to get potatoes?"

"That was the first thing on the list! What the hell am I supposed to do about dinner now?"

"Can I get them on the way home?"

"No! I was going to fix stew in the slow cooker, but I don't have potatoes! How could you forget them?"

"I didn't know what you were making or I would've remembered them."

"Oh, now it's *my* fault they're not here!"

"No, apparently it's *my* fault they're not there. Look, don't sweat it. We can go out."

"No, we can't. This is gaming night for you and I know well enough that you're not going to want to go out. And I don't have what I need to fix dinner. So what the hell are we supposed to do now?"

"We can still go out, baby! It's okay. Don't—"

"I know, I know. Don't sweat it. I'd love to stop for them myself, but you know I can't do that. I don't know what's wrong with you that you couldn't remember a simple bag of potatoes, but it—"

"Whoa! Hold up there, girl! You're about to say some things you're going to regret."

"I doubt it! I'll talk to you later. Bye." She didn't wait for him to say another word, just ended the call and tossed the phone on the counter. *Now* what was she supposed to do? No dinner, he wouldn't want to go out … What a mess. What a fucking, ridiculous mess that she couldn't even go to the store.

Jerrica finished getting ready for work, fuming the whole time. Matter of fact, her shoes made her mad, her jewelry made her mad, and she was mad at her scrubs by the time she got them on. Every damn thing in that house made her mad, and she was furious when she got into the car. As usual, she turned on the radio and she'd just pulled onto the four-lane when she heard something that almost made her slam on her brakes.

"It's the morning commute with Jay and Ray. Hey, we've got a request this morning coming from one of the firefighters at Station Two. Jerrica, if you're listening, this is from Landon. It's Jerrod Niemann and *God Made a Woman,* right here on your morning commute, The Triple D, WDDD, your home for today's country."

It was a simple tune with simple words, but they resonated in Jerrica's chest and she had to pull off the road. She couldn't see for the tears filling her eyes and streaming down her face. Hands shaking, she pulled out her phone and hit his contact. That smooth, deep voice vibrated in her ear. "Hey, baby."

"Oh, god, Landon!" she cried out. "I'm so sorry! I was just so mad, and I needed the potatoes, and—"

"Hold up, babe! Just stop! It's okay! We'll go out and get something, and we can—"

"But gaming—"

"Don't you think I can miss gaming one night to eat dinner with my best girl?"

Jerrica's heart thudded into her stomach. That one night—it was the only thing Landon did for himself all week long, and he was willing to give it up just to have dinner with her somewhere. "I'm so sorry, baby."

"Hey, I can pick up something on my way home. It's okay. I know you're getting moody and—"

That hit Jerrica in just the wrong place at the wrong time. "What do you mean, I'm getting moody?" she asked, bitterness in her voice.

"Your cycle." She sat there, not quite believing what she was hearing. "It's about that time in your cycle, right?"

Was he talking about what she *thought* he was talking about? "My cycle? You mean—"

"Yes. That's exactly what I mean."

"But how do you—"

"How do I know? Babe, it's my job to be there for you and to watch out for you. I pay attention to these things. What kind of boyfriend would I be if I didn't know that?"

She couldn't believe it. He'd figured out her cycle. "Um, a boyfriend like the rest of the boyfriends in the world."

And there it was—that slow, rich chuckle that rumbled out of his chest and warmed her from head to toe. "I'm not like other boyfriends, babe. I'm *your* boyfriend, and I'm trying to be in tune with *you*. I heard a minister say that once on the radio, that if you wanted to really understand your woman, you should pay attention to things like that. I took it to heart. Do other guys not do that?"

"No. Other guys do not."

"Then I guess you got the weird one," he said, chuckling again.

"No. I got the best one. I really am sorry, Landon. I shouldn't have called you and blasted you."

"We need a message center in the kitchen, and you should start writing down lists for me. I can't remember everything."

"You're right."

He laughed aloud. "Can I get that in writing?"

That made Jerrica laugh. "Smartass! If you'll pick up potatoes today, I'll put it in the slow cooker for tomorrow night."

"I'll do that. And baby?"

"Yeah?"

"Are you talking to me while you're driving?"

"No. I had to pull over because I was crying when I heard that song."

"Then get your ass back on the road. You're a sitting duck for anybody who could be following you."

"Oh, god! You're right! Okay, I'm headed to work now. I love you."

She could almost feel his smile when he said, "I love you too."

* * *

"Miss, could we have a word?" Jerrica turned to see two

uniformed police officers standing about two feet from her.

"Me?"

"Yes, ma'am. Please. You're Jerrica Ligon, right?"

"Yes, sir."

"Is there a conference room or something where we could—"

"Just step in here." She led them into one of the ER cubicles and slid the glass door closed. "How can I help you?"

"You were working with Dr. Fielding when he called us to make a report, correct?"

"Yes, sir."

"Could you tell us everything you observed?"

"Sure." Jerrica went into as much detail as she could, trying to remember. She was still angry with herself because she never really looked at the men's faces. She'd been too concerned with the burns the injured one had to be interested in what they looked like. "And I'm sorry I don't know more."

"You've given us quite a bit. Do you think you'd recognize them if you saw them?"

That pang of regret slipped back into her chest. "No, sir. I was so busy looking at the burns that I didn't pay attention to their faces. Wish I had. Do you think it was one of them?"

"We don't know. There wasn't anything taken from Dr. Fielding and no signs of a struggle. As far as we can tell, he had no enemies, no disgruntled patients, and he and his wife were getting along fine. Nothing seemed to be wrong there. The person or people seemed pretty savvy about avoiding the security cameras, so the recordings have given us nothing. We're following any lead we can find because we really have nothing to work with."

"He was a very nice man. When I was doing my ER rotation here in nursing school, he actually came in and helped me with my homework one day. A very nice man, and a very compassionate doctor." Tears sprang to her eyes. She hadn't allowed herself to think about it much, but now that she had a chance to, she knew she'd miss him. He always told corny jokes and brought cookies his wife had made to the break room.

"I'm sorry for your loss, ma'am. We'll let you get back to your work. Thanks for your time."

"Quite all right. I'm glad to help if I can. My boyfriend is a firefighter and—"

The other officer turned and smiled. "Oh, yeah? Who is he?"

"Landon Fox?"

"Yeah! We know Hose! He makes our lives miserable every year at the Cops and Firefighters Football Tournament. Helluva football player, that one!"

"So I've heard! I'll tell him I met you, Officer—"

"Just tell him Jamie and Taylor. He'll know who you're talking about. Thanks again, and good to meet you, Jerrica."

"You too." She watched them make their way across

the parking lot and wondered if they'd ever catch whoever had killed Dr. Fielding. And what about the downtown fires? Had any of the law enforcement divisions realized something was going on? Probably not, or not yet anyway. She hoped Landon could help the FBI figure it all out. Time was running out.

And somebody else was bound to get hurt.

* * *

They stood in the shadow of the sheriff's department's building and waited. In a couple of minutes, the kid came out and ambled toward them. "Well?"

"No, sir. Not there."

"Good. Here's your twenty. Don't spend it all in one place."

"Thanks, mister." They watched as he climbed on his bike and rode away.

The man with burns on his arms pulled his sleeves down farther on the tops of his hands and shivered. "Well, they don't have our pictures or a sketch up. That's good news."

"Yeah, it means that woman hasn't been able to identify us, but it's only a matter of time. She's always got somebody with her unless she's driving, and we can't chase her down."

"When she does describe us, we're fucked."

"Don't worry," the guy without the burns said. "She's gotta slip up sometime."

* * *

"You off tomorrow?" Jerrica asked as they unpacked all the Chinese takeout Landon had brought home.

"Yeah. And there's something I wanted to talk to you about."

"Oh, shit. Here it comes. I said I was sorry," she mumbled.

"No, not that! I'm having a security system put in the house. I really think we need it, especially if you're going to be here alone for any length of time."

She nodded as she took plates out of the cabinet. "I think you're right. I'd feel a lot better that way."

"Yeah, and I'm getting one that's not hardwired. It would be easy to disable one of those, but one that runs on an air card? No. That would be almost impossible to defeat."

"Good thinking. What is that, mu shu pork?"

"Yeah. Here." Landon handed her the carton. "They'll be here tomorrow to put it in. We need to talk about codes before you leave for work and decide on a couple. By the way, I think I've come up with a way to find out what's going on with the downtown fires."

"Yeah? How?"

Landon outlined the idea and Jerrica agreed. It sounded like it would work if there really was something going on. Putting it in play wouldn't be hard at all. Just a couple of phone calls and maybe they'd know the truth.

* * *

There were three main real estate offices in Taylorsville, and between them they had about eighteen agents, but there was one Landon knew well.

"Hey, Dan, how's it going? Landon Fox here."

"Landon! How ya doin'? You looking for property?"

"Maybe, maybe. Thought I'd ask before buyers are lined up."

"Oh! You've got a particular property picked out?"

"Yes and no. You know all the fires we've been having downtown?"

"Yeah?"

"Well, I have to believe some of those owners want to offload that property."

There was silence for a few seconds before Dan asked, "What in the world would you want with that?"

"I was thinking maybe I'd be part of the revitalization. We need to bring downtown back."

"Very true. So which piece of property?"

"That part doesn't matter. Just thought I'd check and see if any of it was available."

"And what are you planning to put on it?" Dan asked.

Landon snickered. When people thought of cops, they thought of donuts. He knew what they thought of when they thought of firefighters. "A barbecue place."

"Oh! Wouldn't that be perfect? Let me see what I can find out and give you a call back. Give me your number." Landon recited it and Dan said, "Got it. You'll hear from me as soon as I know something."

"Great. Sounds good. I'll be waiting." Landon ended the call and stood there staring at his phone. That was all he knew to do.

It was almost time for dinner that evening when Landon's phone rang, and he recognized the number as the real estate office. "Hello?"

"Landon! Glad I caught you. Hey, I did a little digging and you won't believe this. Three of the lots are already sold."

Boy, they didn't waste any time! "Seriously? To whom?"

"I dunno. Some outfit called KMM Holdings."

"Who's that?"

"No idea. They're not local. I've never heard of them before. But I did find you a property that's not gone yet, although the owner told me he'd gotten an offer from those guys."

"Hmmm. Which property?"

"Two twenty-two." Landon recognized the number immediately—it was the last building that had burned. "They contacted him this morning. Said they got his info from records at the courthouse."

Was that what the arsonists were doing when they weren't setting fires? Scoping out the records at the courthouse? That should make it easy enough to catch them. "Okay, well, tell the owner I'm interested in that property and I want to know what they offer so I can counter." If the owner told those people he had another buyer, they'd be furious. That would slow them down a bit.

"Will do. I'll call him right back."

"Hey, Dan, can you tell me—did they buy all those properties at the same time, or did they buy them one by one?"

"Uh, let me look at the dates ... One by one, and about a week after each one burned, so they've been looking for property this whole time. Come to think of it, that *is* kinda odd. Do you think—"

"Gotta go, Dan. Thanks for the info and keep me posted about that property. Bye." *You can't say a word to him,* Landon told himself. It had to be kept quiet, but there was one person he'd sure tell.

Agent Cruz Livingston was getting a call that evening. It couldn't wait.

* * *

Jerrica listened as Landon talked to Cruz and filled him in on everything he'd found out. The whole thing was creepy, and she couldn't figure out why anybody would want that property. It was in an old section of town, nowhere near the amenities at the outskirts. As property went, it was probably cheap. Maybe that was the draw.

When Landon hung up, Jerrica propped her elbows on the counter of the island in their big kitchen. "So?

What did he say?"

"He said he's going to use his contacts to see if he can find out who this KMM Holdings is. He said he's seen some scams run through holding companies, but nothing like this. I hope he comes up with something."

"You really think the arsonists are going to the courthouse and looking up the titles?"

"How else are these owners getting calls from this place? It's not like every piece of property has an I.D. tag on it. It takes some sleuthing to find out who they belong to, and so far, every owner has been located and an offer made to them. There's just one problem."

"What's that?"

"They're about to run out of vacant properties to burn. It won't be long before they'll have to start burning occupied buildings, and that's a whole different ballgame. There'll be insurance companies to deal with and claims agents, and all of that."

"Have the inspector's and marshal's reports come back yet?"

"No, and I forgot to mention that to Cruz. That's kinda fishy. They should've been in weeks ago. I'm beginning to wonder if they're in on it."

"I suppose it's possible." Jerrica picked up the dish towel and folded it neatly before placing it on the countertop beside the sink. "I think I'm ready for bed. What about you?"

Landon grinned. "Oh, I'm past ready!"

"Good. Let's go."

Thirty minutes later, Jerrica was gasping. Everything about Landon, every touch of his hand, every tweak of her nipples, every inch of his hardness, turned her on more than she'd ever been turned on in her life. She loved watching his muscles ripple as he stroked into her, and the stretch and burn were the things of which fantasies were made. "Harder, baby, please?"

"Jesus, babe, I pound you much harder and your head will whack the headboard!" he said with a snicker.

"I don't care. Harder, baby. I need it."

"Yes, ma'am," he said, his voice breathy as he bent down to kiss her. When he broke the kiss, he began stroking her clit as he pounded into her. "I love you, Jerrica. And dear god, I love to fuck you. Girl, you are one amazing ride."

"You are too, stud. I love you, Landon. I can't get enough of you."

"Good, because we're just getting started, gorgeous. You look amazing, babe, just amazing. How the hell am I supposed to make this last with you looking all crazy sexy like that, hmmm? I'm about to top off your tank, sweetheart. Just … uhhhh, yeah. Just. Like. Ahhhhh—that!" She could feel it, the heat and wetness of the one thing only he could give her, and Jerrica smiled. Someday he'd do that and her belly would get round and full. She'd give him a son or a daughter who'd look like him, all beautiful and tanned and dark-haired. Or a little girl with blond curls and big blue eyes like hers. Wouldn't that be amazing?

He lay on top of her, panting, his arms around her, and she gripped his neck tightly. "I love you, Landon. I want to make a home and babies with you."

"Someday soon I want to make a home and babies with you too. But for now, we'll have to wait on the babies, I guess. Did you get what you need?"

"Three times! Couldn't you tell?"

"I was a little busy, darlin'. And holy shit, that second time I thought you were going to levitate right up off the bed!"

She laughed. "I did too! You're very talented, Mr. Fox!"

"And you're very beautiful, future Mrs. Fox." He kissed her, a long, slow thing that wound around her heart like a climbing rose. When he drew back, he smiled. "I have never in my life been as happy as I am right now."

"I feel the same way. Sometimes I think I'll die of happiness."

"Don't do that! I won't be happy by myself!"

He dropped onto the mattress beside her and she rolled to her side to face him. "I wasn't happy by myself."

His voice was soft and warm when he said, "I wasn't happy by myself either. I'm so glad I'm not by myself anymore."

"I'm glad I'm not by myself too. But you do realize … I've seen your parents. When you're eighty, you'll still be tall and gorgeous. Your dad is barely sixty and he's a good-looking man. But you've seen my mother. That's what I'm going to look like, Landon, short and round and plain. Are you sure you're still going to want me when I look like that?"

He kissed the tip of her nose, then ran his fingers through her hair to push it away from her face. "You're my girl. No matter how long we're together, what we look like, or what happens to us, you're still my girl. Always. My best girl. My only girl. We have a daughter, you'll *still* be my best girl, because long after she's grown, you'll still be with me. We're all we've got, baby, and I'm perfectly okay with that."

Jerrica snuggled into Landon's chest and sighed as his arms tightened around her. There, in those strong arms, she felt cherished, loved, and protected. She couldn't stay there all the time, but she tried to commit that feeling to memory. It was the best thing in her life; *he* was the best thing in her life. Nothing could ever be any better.

Nothing.

* * *

Landon was helping Stingray and Tinman work on one of the trucks when his phone rang. It was a Louisville number he didn't recognize, but something told him to answer it anyway. "Hello?"

"Is this Landon Fox?"

"Yes. Can I help you?"

"Mr. Fox, this is Special Agent Bob Clark in the FBI's Louisville office. Is this a good time for you to talk?"

"It can be." Landon excused himself and headed to the kitchen of the firehouse. "Okay. I'm alone. Can I help you?"

"I got a call from Agent Livingston in San Antonio and he told me a very interesting story. He decided to pass this on to us, but let me thank you in advance for putting yourself out there. This could be dangerous for anyone who knows about it. Can you tell me who you've talked to about this?"

"Just a friend who's a deputy, Agent Livingston, and my girlfriend."

"Uh, Jerrica Ligon?"

"Yes, sir."

"And no one else?"

"No, sir. I called the real estate agent, but he thinks I'm going to put in a barbecue restaurant. I told him nothing."

"Good. That's good. Is there anything else you've thought of, anything at all, that you might be able to tell me? I mean, Agent Livingston's notes are pretty solid, but I wondered if there was anything you've come up with."

"Actually, yeah, there is something I forgot. We've never gotten the fire inspector's or fire marshal's reports on the fires, and honestly, I think that's pretty odd."

"Are you saying you think they could be involved?"

"I'm saying I'm afraid they might be."

"And do you know these men well?"

"No. I only know them in passing. They sometimes come around and talk to the captain, but that's about it. Most of the time we don't even see them."

"I see. Do you know their names?"

"Yeah. The inspector is Michael Averett and the marshal is Greg Yates."

"Good. Would it bother you if I called your captain?"

"No, sir, but I'd appreciate it if you'd let me give him a heads-up first. We all trust each other around here, and I don't want him to think I'm trying to pull something on him."

"Of course. I understand. Have you heard back from the real estate agent yet?"

"No, sir. He's trying to get me a price on the newest property that's become available. I'm waiting until he can do that."

"Gotcha. Let me know when he does and what he says, if you don't mind. The number I called you from is my office number, but I'll give you my cell number. Feel free to call me at any time, and I do mean at any time. I realize you're a firefighter, but to us you're a civilian, and we don't want you or your girlfriend in harm's way." He rattled off his number and Landon scratched it down on a napkin.

"Thank you, sir. I appreciate that. I suppose Agent Livingston told you she saw the arsonists."

"He did, but he said she didn't get a good look at their faces."

"That's right. Now we're scared they'll come after her."

"It's a very real possibility. I'd take every precaution if I were you."

"We're trying to, sir. Thank you, Special Agent Clark."

"You're quite welcome. Thank you for your cooperation. And for the record, it's just Bob. Hope it'll be all right if I call you Landon."

"Of course. Not a problem. Thanks, Bob, and as soon as the real estate agent calls me, I'll call you."

"Great. Have a good evening, Landon, and we'll talk soon." The phone went silent and Landon placed it on the counter.

Now the FBI really was involved. That should've made him feel better. Instead, it made him more afraid. And his biggest fear was that the killers would come after Jerrica.

* * *

Landon had decided he was just going to have to call Dan himself when his phone rang. "Hey, Dan!"

"Landon! Good news. I've got the amount for you. They offered eleven thousand."

"That's all?"

"Yeah. For a small property in a depressed area, that's really a pretty good offer, seeing as how they'll have to clean it up themselves."

"I guess so. Hey, I hate that you went to all that trouble, but I talked it over with my girlfriend and she said seeing as how we're going to be getting married, she—"

"You're getting married? Congratulations! When's the happy day?"

"Haven't decided yet. Anyway, she said she thought this would be a lousy time for me to try to do something like this, so I think I'm going to pass after all. Maybe a year or two down the road—"

"Say no more. I understand, and when you get ready, I'm sure I'll have a piece of property for you! Maybe some more buildings will burn down between now and then!" Dan said and laughed. Landon didn't think that was funny—at all.

"Who knows? But yeah, thanks, Dan. Talk to you in a year or so." Landon hit END before he could lose his cool. Who said something like that? Someone who was ignorant of all the risks involved in putting out a fire like that. Dan couldn't help it. He didn't understand that Carlos had lost his life doing that. It was just another fire to him.

He didn't waste any time calling Special Agent Clark. "Bob Clark here."

"Bob, this is Landon Fox."

"I take it you heard back from the realtor?"

"Yes. Eleven thousand. That's what they've offered, and I'm betting the owner will take it. It's a depressed area and they'll have to pay for cleanup if they don't sell it."

"Gotcha. I hope you gave him a good excuse for not buying it."

"Yep. Told him I'm getting married and my girlfriend thought it would be a lousy time to do it."

"Good. Now, I've got some news for you, and it's not good."

Landon swallowed hard. "Yes, sir?"

"We started digging around on KMM Holdings. Landon, this is a wide-spread thing. They've got properties in several states, but they've been doing this in a couple of towns in Texas, one in Arkansas, three in Alabama, one in Kentucky—yours—that we know of, and two in Tennessee. It appears they're going in, burning buildings, then buying up the properties. Same kind of pattern, all in a small geographical area."

"But why?"

"Government-subsidized housing. They build huge apartment complexes with partial government funding. It brings low-income residents into the downtown areas, and that effectively shuts off revitalization prospects. That means that, later on, they can buy up even more property in those towns. In the towns in Arkansas, they have eight city blocks of subsidized housing downtown. The first four they acquired by burning. The others they acquired because it starved the property owners out. They couldn't get businesses to move in, so they sold and walked away."

"Holy shit."

"Yeah. Holy shit is right. This is a huge scheme. Based on what we know, that means they've hired arsonists in virtually every state to do their dirty work. It's a big operation, Landon. Somebody's going to get hurt, and if anybody gets in their way, they'll eliminate them. That's what happened to Dr. Fielding."

"Is there organized crime money involved in this?"

"We're checking on that too. But for now, you need to be careful, especially with your girlfriend. She's truly in danger."

"Yes, sir. I had a security system put in."

"Hope it has some panic buttons. You may need them."

"It does. Thanks for talking to me, Bob. If I find out anything else, I'll let you know."

"Sure thing. And talk to your captain tomorrow. I'll call him in two days, so I wanted to give you a chance to get that out of the way."

"Will do. Thanks. Bye." The knot of burning bile in his chest grew larger. Jerrica was in danger. The idea of anyone hurting her cut him to the quick. *Maybe I should send her away to Beth and Cade's or somewhere. I don't like this at all.* He knew how that would go. She'd fight him bloody over that idea. Besides, he really didn't want her going anywhere, but he couldn't watch her all the time.

Landon didn't know what to do, but he knew one thing.

Letting Jerrica get hurt wasn't an option.

* * *

"I can't do this. I need an antibiotic or something," the man croaked out as he lay on the sofa. The burns on his arms had blackened, and his partner was pretty sure they were gangrenous. "Can't you just take me to a clinic or something?"

"No, dumbass. If we do that, they'll start questioning you and we'll get caught. You'll just have to tough it out."

"But I can't. I'm really sick, man." The guy named James looked at his arms. They didn't look right, he knew. "Please, I need help, Rick."

"I told you, no. Not happening. I've got to get something out of the car. Be right back." Rick walked out the door of the little motel room, closed it behind him, and stepped around the corner after glancing around to make sure no one was near. He hit a contact in his phone and waited.

A voice answered, "This had better be important."

"It is. This dumb motherfucker is going to die on me, man. You're going to have to find me another partner."

"That wasn't part of the deal. You want to get paid, you'll carry out the instructions."

"But I can't do all this by myself!"

"Should've thought about that before you let him get hurt."

"*Let* him get hurt! You hired him and he was too stupid to know what he was doing! Besides, we couldn't have known there'd be pockets of gas in that building!"

"Look, the two of you are going to keep on until we get caught at this, and the whole thing will fall like a house of cards. I've got notes coming due and I've got to have the money to pay them, so these things have to get built pretty damn fast. Have you gotten all the buildings taken down?"

"No. One of them is a daycare."

"I don't give a god damn if it's a nunnery, I want those buildings burned to the ground by the end of next week, do you hear me?"

"Yes, sir. I hear you. I'll get it done." Without another word, he hung up and made his way back inside. James was barely breathing, lying on the sofa with his eyes closed. *If he dies on me, I'll just dump his body. Maybe I can find a place where nobody will find it.* He could sink it in Taylorsville Lake. No one would find it there.

No one would be looking for it.

CHAPTER 8

"Sir?"

"Fox! Come on in. What's up?"

"I need to talk to you about something." Landon glanced back at the doorway.

"Sure. Close it. Now, what's going on?" Captain Martin asked as he motioned for Landon to sit.

"You're going to get a call from the FBI. I just wanted to give you a heads-up. You know, so you won't be blindsided."

"What's going on?"

Landon spent the next twenty minutes explaining to Captain Martin what he'd discovered and what the FBI had discovered as well. The captain's eyes grew wider and wider until finally Landon said, "Well, what do you think?"

"I think you're pretty damn sharp, Hose. And I think you're onto something."

"So I was hoping you could lean on the inspector and marshal and see what happens."

"I'll do just that and let you know. What's this agent's name?"

"Special Agent Bob Clark. Nice guy."

"Good. I'll be expecting his call. Thanks for telling me. Now, you take care of that girl. Jerrica seems like a sweetheart, and I don't want to see anything happen to her."

"Yes, sir. I'm doing all I can."

"Don't be afraid to ask some of the guys to come over and stay with her if you can't be there. I know they wouldn't mind."

Landon laughed. "That's what I'm afraid of, sir!" At Captain Martin's laughter, Landon said, "I'm just kidding. I know none of them would do that to me."

"Nah. But they'd think about it, you know they would!" That set Landon laughing again, mostly because he knew the captain was right.

"Seriously, sir, thanks for reminding me. I'll ask some of them if I'm not going to be home. That's a pretty good idea." It really was. There was one thing he knew for sure.

He'd give his life for Jerrica. And if he asked any of his brothers from the firehouse to watch over her, they'd do the same.

* * *

As soon as she got home, Jerrica locked the back door and set the alarm. Then she went to the front door and peered out. Nothing was moving, and she was glad once again that they had a garage that opened into the house. She could drive in, put the door down, and she was safely inside their little world.

Twenty minutes later, she heard the garage door go up again and froze. It was bound to be Landon, but what if … "Babe? You here?" she heard his voice call out. As soon as she reached him, he grabbed her hands and stared down at her. "Why are you shaking?"

"I wasn't sure if it was you."

"Jerr, honey, nobody else has an opener for our garage."

"What if somebody figured out the code and opened it from outside?"

Landon sighed. "Jerrica, we've had this discussion before. You're safe here. We've got alarms everywhere—entry alarms, glass breakage alarms, panic buttons. I know you're spooked, but it's okay. You'll be fine here, I promise."

"But what if I'm not?"

"Babe, I—" He was interrupted by a knock at the door. "Who in the world is that?" At the front door, he peered through the peephole, then threw the door open. "Blane! What the hell?"

"Is your girlfriend here?"

"Jerrica? Yeah. What's—"

"Can I talk to her for a minute?"

"Sure. Why is the coroner's van—"

Jerrica appeared at Landon's elbow. "What's going on?"

"Could you come out here and take a look? Lady out walking found a body off of Westminster Road and we're wondering if this is one of our arsonists."

"Uh, yeah, okay. I'll look." Jerrica started out the door, but Landon grabbed her arm. "What?"

"Are you sure you want to do this?"

She rolled her eyes. "No. But if it helps catch these guys, then yes, I'll do it." In seconds she was following Blane down the walk and out toward the van. The deputy coroner got out, opened the back door, and unzipped the body bag. Jerrica took one look and nodded. "Yep. That's him."

"Okay. At least we know we have one of them. The other one is still at large. Thanks. I'm sorry to have to ask you to do this."

"It's okay. Part of the process, I suppose. Glad I could be of help." Jerrica and Landon stood and watched as the coroner's van pulled away with Blane's cruiser right behind it. "Well, that's that."

"Yeah, we don't know where the other one is, but we know where that one is. He won't be bothering anybody."

"But doesn't that make the other one more dangerous?"

Landon sighed. "Yeah, probably."

"Great. Just great." Things only seemed to go from bad to worse, and Jerrica had started to wonder if she'd make it to see herself married to the man beside her.

* * *

Two weeks went by with silence, and Landon started to wonder if they'd given up. He let Jerrica go to the grocery a couple of times by herself, but most of the time he went with her. It was broad daylight. What could happen?

He was pulling an overnighter and had insisted she stay with her parents for the night. She'd gotten mad, but he told her it was that or he was sending Stingray and Red over to stay with her. Suddenly, her parents' house sounded pretty good, and that made Landon laugh. He and the guys settled down for a few games of five-card stud, betting with salted peanuts in the shell, when the tone went off. "Station Two, Station Two, respond to structure fire, one eighteen East First Street. Repeat, respond to structure fire, one eighteen East First Street. Copy?"

Tinman hit the button on the radio console. "Copy that, central dispatch. Station Two responding." Everyone else had donned their turnout gear, and he was the last to join them on the rig. As they tore out of the firehouse, Mater glanced over at Landon. "You realize that's St. Xavier Church, right?"

Landon's chest constricted. Thank god it was late at night and no one was there, but to know someone had set fire to that old building was heartbreaking, and he was sure that was the case. Of course, it could be faulty wiring, but he was betting it wasn't. What would they find when they got there?

A disaster. His chest tightened in grief as they raced up to the perimeter and took a look at the building. It was fully engulfed, the old terra cotta roofing tiles popping and cracking from the heat and the lead melting from the big stained glass windows. So much history, a place where so many people in that town had been baptized, married, and memorialized, that it was hard to picture the city without it. The voices around him seemed to be mere echoes until somebody slapped him on the shoulder. "Lieu!"

"Uh, yeah, you guys get your respirators on. We're going to make sure there's nobody in there. Who called this in?"

"I don't know," a police officer standing nearby said. "We got the call and came down to set a perimeter for you guys."

From seemingly out of nowhere, a nun came running up the street. "Oh, dear Lord! Dear Lord! Father Dumfree!"

Landon wheeled toward the sound of her voice. "Sister, where is Father Dumfree?"

"He'd gone to the church to retrieve some papers!

We were having a meeting in the rectory and it ran long. Oh, dear Lord! He's in the building somewhere!"

"You two," Landon ordered Bobo and a guy they called Flea, "you're coming with me. Let's go." Landon pried open the side door of the church and peered inside. Smoke filled the hallways as they made their way up the stairs. He motioned for Bobo to head into the offices on the left and he and Flea proceeded to the stairs, took the seven steps, and found their way into the sanctuary. Everything seemed in order there until Flea poked him in the shoulder and he turned. The younger man pointed toward the confessional, and when Landon took a second look, he saw something that made his heart stop.

A foot.

Rushing to the confessional, he threw back the curtain and what he found there stunned him. It was Father Dumfree—with a knife in his chest. Landon checked, but there was no pulse, and he hit the mic on his respirator. "We've got the priest here. I need three men and a stretcher in the front doors of the sanctuary. We'll open them from the inside. Bobo, evacuate."

"Roger that, lieu."

Landon and Flea opened the huge wooden doors to find three more firefighters standing there with a litter. Without a word, he directed them to the confessional and helped them load up the priest. The smoke was getting thicker, but the trucks were hampered in their ability to pour water in as long as the men were inside.

"Let's get out of here," he said and pointed toward the doors, and all five men made their way out of the building, carrying the priest's lifeless body with them.

Captain Martin had gotten the call and driven there, and when he saw the priest on the litter he shook his head. "Oh, my god. I don't believe this. Hose?"

Landon ripped the respirator from his face. "Yes, Captain?"

"I take it you found him that way?"

"Yes, sir, Flea did. I wanted to remove the body in case the building couldn't be salvaged. The smoke's getting pretty bad, and I'd say we're not going to have a lot of luck fighting this, seeing as how it's started above and there's limited access."

"I think that was a good call. Tell your men to knock out the upstairs windows and get all the water in there that they can."

Landon held the respirator up to his face and pushed the button on his comm unit. "Two men on each side! Knock those windows out and start that pumper truck!"

"But, lieu ..." he heard over his headset.

"I know, I know. Do it anyway." They were balking at the idea of destroying the beautiful stained glass windows. The idea made him sick too, but none of that mattered in the moment. "Skeeter, Wheels, on the east side; Spider, Bandit, on the west side." He could hear the pumps start up on the truck and knew they'd have water for at least a little while. "Ranger, get those hydrants open! Station Three, you copy?"

"Station Three, over."

"We could use some help on the north end of the building. You have access to all hydrants. Lieutenant Masters, do you copy?"

"Gotcha, Lieutenant Fox." He listened as Station Three's lieutenant gave orders to his men for positions and jobs, and watched as everyone worked together.

"Could I have a word?" Landon heard someone say and turned to find Terry Morris, a Taylorsville Police Department sergeant, standing right beside him.

"Sure."

"Where exactly did you find his body?"

"Flea was the one who noticed it first. His foot was sticking out of the confessional."

"He was in the *confessional*?"

"Yep."

"Wow. Talk about having no respect."

Landon nodded. "I thought the same thing. I took his pulse immediately and I knew he was already gone."

"This is the second stabbing we've had."

"Yeah. Dr. Fielding."

"Do you think they're related?" Terry asked.

Landon nodded again. "I *know* they're related."

"Wish we could preserve the crime scene."

"Unfortunately, I think you're going to lose that, but I carried him out so at least you'd have whatever physical evidence might be on the body and the weapon."

"That's good. Crime lab and coroner will process all that. Thanks, Landon."

"You're welcome." He watched Terry walk away and thought about all the parishioners. They would be devastated at the loss of their priest and their house of worship. The building was one of the oldest in Taylorsville and could never be replaced, not to mention all the items inside that were antique and had been given in honor or memory of loved ones by the town's families over the years. Those would be lost too. Sure enough, in mere seconds he heard Skeeter yell through his headset, "We're losing the first floor!" just before it crashed into the basement. Sparks shot out every window and the men lurched backward to avoid them, then took up their stations again.

Another property. Only the library branch and the daycare remained. If whoever had burned the church had no problem stabbing a priest to death, he wouldn't have any problem killing innocent children. Landon didn't want to inspire panic, but he knew he had to do something. Just sitting and waiting for the FBI to act wasn't an option. He had to talk to the captain to figure out how to approach it, but the other properties' occupants needed to know the danger they were facing.

They worked until three thirty the next morning trying to put out all the hot spots and by the time they were finished, Landon was exhausted. Another shift came in to take over and pack up all the gear so they could leave, and Landon was glad to go. He drove home, the smell of smoke still in his hair, and when he got there, he was greeted with the darkness and silence of the house. After taking a quick shower, he dragged on a pair of boxer briefs and crawled into bed.

His eyes closed and he sighed. *Fuck, I miss my girl.* Grabbing her pillow, he held it to his face and breathed in the scent of her shampoo. It was almost unbearable, being there without her, and he picked up his phone and texted her. She was asleep, but at least she'd see it when she got up in the morning and got ready for work at her parents' house. *Hey, baby. Just want you to know I'm okay and I miss you like crazy. Love you. XOXO*

His phone had no more come to rest on the nightstand when it pinged, and he picked it up and smiled. *I miss you too and I love you. XOXO*

What are you doing awake? he texted back.

Can't sleep without you beside me.

That made him laugh. *That's bad for a firefighter's wife!*

He laughed even harder when he got hers back: *I'm not a firefighter's wife YET!*

We're going to change that, he shot back.

Good. I'll hold you to that. Goodnight, babe. See you when I get off work. Love you.

See you then, beautiful. Love you too. Goodnight.

Landon put his phone back on the nightstand and smiled there alone in the darkness. She couldn't sleep without him. That was cute. And also bad for a nurse. But what the hell—at least she missed him!

It only took him a few minutes to fall asleep, but when he did, he had a nightmare about the priest wandering around in the burning church with the knife sticking out of his chest and all the parishioners screaming and crying. When he woke, sunlight was streaming in around the curtains and he could hear birds singing outside. But deep down inside his soul, there was a blackness.

And it was pure fear.

* * *

Jerrica hit the door and ran straight into Landon's arms. "Oh, my god, I missed you!"

He gripped her tightly to him. "I missed you too! I'm glad you're home."

"Me too. Tell me what happened last night! The priest was killed?"

"Come sit down with me and I'll tell you the whole story, but first, go get out of your scrubs, put on something comfortable, and I'll pour you a glass of wine."

"Oooo, sounds good! I'll be back in a second." He hated to have to tell her everything that had happened. It was a terrible tale waiting to be told, and he wanted to spare her, but there was no way to do that.

She came wandering back into the den in a pair of cute little pajamas and her slippers. "Here, babe. Enjoy," Landon told her as he set her glass of wine down and sat down beside her. After being on her feet all day, there was nothing she liked better than a good foot rub, and he didn't mind having that job one bit. "So here's what happened."

When he finished, Jerrica set her half-empty wine glass down on the table. "Good lord, Landon. That's horrible."

"Yeah, and then I had a nightmare about it."

"Oh, babe, I'm sorry. What about the daycare and the library?"

Landon shrugged. "I don't know what to do about that. I'll talk to the captain about it. Maybe he can—" The ringing of his phone interrupted him and he glanced at the screen. "Hey, Bob."

"Hello, Landon. I just heard the news. They stabbed the priest?"

"Yep. Right in the chest. Knew exactly what they were doing. I guess by now you listened to my message and know one of them was found dead the other day."

"Yes, and I must say, if they'd stab a priest, that was too good for that son of a bitch. These are ruthless people we're dealing with. I guess they'll get yet another parcel of land."

"Maybe not," Landon said with a grin. "There are two bishops and a local cardinal buried beneath the foundation of the church. Those people aren't going to want to give that land up."

"Oh, wow! I'll say not! That could turn ugly quickly. What about the other properties?"

"I really don't know how to approach them, but I'm going to let the captain help me figure it out."

"Whatever you decide, I'm sure it'll be the right thing. The safety of anyone on those properties is of the utmost importance now."

"Agreed. If I hear anything else, I'll let you know."

"Please do. And I'm sorry about the church. I know it was a landmark in your community. It's a sad day."

"It is. Thank you. I'll be in touch." Landon ended the call and laid the phone gently on the coffee table. "This has to end."

"It will when they've burned down everything they need to burn down. But there won't be anything left of the town at the rate they're going." Jerrica took another swallow of wine and looked up at Landon. "I'm sorry this has fallen on you, babe."

"It is what it is." Fingers kneading and pressing, he massaged her feet and thought about the whole predicament. Maybe it was almost over. Maybe they'd burn down the rest while they were unoccupied and it would finally stop. But at what cost?

* * *

He watched from behind the bushes as the woman walked to her car, a security guard right behind her. The parking lot was quiet, with only a person here or there wandering around. They rounded the corner of the building and he made his move while there was no one else in proximity to her car. The knife slipped into the guard's back easily enough and before she could scream, he clapped the rag over her mouth and nose and waited until she slumped against him. Then he put the pillowcase over her head, tied it around her neck, took her keys from her hand, and stuffed her in the trunk. In seconds, he'd started her car and driven away.

Driving well within the speed limit so as not to draw attention, he moved around the city, pulling in here and there as though he were shopping or something. When he was convinced no one was wise to him, he drove straight to the house, opened the garage door, drove the car in, and closed the door behind it. That stupid ass James couldn't do anything right. He'd have to do it all. Lifting her out of the trunk, he dumped her on the floor and dragged her by her feet across the room and into a small closet, then tied her hands together and left her on the floor, closing the door behind him.

He could've killed her. He knew that. But he had a better plan for getting rid of the meddlesome bitch. "Call it poetic justice," he mumbled, "but it'll get rid of you once and for all." She'd be terrified when she woke, and that excited him even more. There'd be no one left who could identify him. All he had to do was complete two more jobs.

And one of them would include her.

* * *

Jerrica woke to a pounding headache and total darkness. The heat was stifling, and she couldn't remember what had happened. She'd been at the hospital, and she remembered Stan Philips walking her out, but nothing after that. Where was she? "Hello? Anybody? Can anybody hear me?"

"Shut up," a voice growled from somewhere nearby. "I don't need to hear your caterwauling. Just be quiet."

Jesus! It's that guy! Jerrica thought, remembering the voice. She'd heard it that day from the other side of the curtain while the two men talked in the cubicle. Dear god, what had he done? "Please, let me out. I couldn't identify you. You know that already. Just let me go and there's no way I can lead them to you. I promise."

"I'm not taking any chances. You just shut up. You're not going to be around long enough to cause me any more trouble."

What did he mean by that? *Oh, god, he's going to kill me,* Jerrica realized. That's what he had in mind. Why hadn't he already done it? "But I don't know who you are! Why have you done this?"

"Because I'm tired of everybody looking for me, that's why. And I've fucking had to work alone since you couldn't fix up my partner, so it'll be your turn soon enough." What did he mean by that? Jerrica shuddered there in the darkness of the closet. Landon would be home soon, and he'd be looking for her. As soon as he realized she was missing, he'd be out everywhere. There was no stone he wouldn't overturn to find her, and this guy was no match for hers.

"You know my boyfriend is going to find you and when he does, he'll kill you. He'll show you no mercy. Are you ready for that?"

"Your boyfriend ain't gonna do diddly-squat. By the time he finds you, there won't be anything left of you."

Oh, my god! He's planning to burn me up! Oh, please, somebody, help me! I've got to get out of here! Jerrica tried the rope holding her hands tight, but there was no use. She couldn't get it loose. *Please, send somebody to help me!* her brain screamed, but there was no reply. He had her and he wasn't planning to let her go. *I love you, Landon,* she sent out to the universe. *I know you'll find me.*

She sure hoped she was right.

* * *

When the garage door opened, Landon was shocked—Jerrica's little car wasn't there. He knew she'd gotten off work before he did, so where was she? He called her cell, but it went to voicemail after it had rung what seemed to be a ridiculous amount of times. Not wanting to cause any hysterics, he called her mother and worked hard to keep his panic at bay. "Hey, Amy, it's Landon."

"Oh, hi, Landon! How are you?"

"I'm good. Is Jerrica there?"

"Uh, no. She's not. I haven't seen her. Why?"

"No reason. I guess she stopped at the store."

"I thought she wasn't supposed to do that by herself," Amy said, suspicion thick in her voice.

"She's not, but I'm sure it was just for one or two things. She'll be home in a minute."

"Okay, well, if you don't hear from her soon, let us know, okay? Please?"

"Yeah, I will. Nothing to worry about. Bye." Where else might she be? He called the salon, but she wasn't there. The only other place was … No. She wouldn't go to his parents' house without him. Would she? His mother answered on the first ring. "Hello?"

"Mom, it's Landon. Is Jerrica there by any chance?"

"Well, no, dear. Why on earth would she be here?"

"I just … I thought she'd beat me home, but she's not here."

"No, son. We haven't seen her. But if I do, I'll give you a call. Landon, is everything okay?"

"No, Mom. Everything's not okay."

"Did you two have a fight?"

"No, Mom. We didn't have a fight. This is far more serious."

"If you decide you want to talk about it, then I'm—"

"Mom, I've got to go. I'll talk to you later. Thanks. Bye." He'd no more than hung up when his phone rang. "Hello?"

"Landon? It's Blane."

"Yeah, what's up?"

"Nothing good. One of the security guards has been

stabbed. He's in surgery right now and they don't know if he's going to make it. And the girl at the desk in the emergency room told us he was walking Jerrica out."

"Is her car there?"

"Red G6, right? No. It's not here."

The room began to spin and it was hard to breathe. "Thanks, Blane. I've gotta go. I've got a call to make." He paged through his contacts until he found the right one.

"Special Agent Clark."

"Bob, this is Landon Fox. They've got Jerrica."

"What? What makes you think that?"

Landon told him everything he knew, and he heard nothing from the other end. "Are you still there?"

"I am. I'm calling the local sheriff's office and the chief of police, and I'll have a team there in a couple of hours. Landon, don't go off the rails here. We'll find her. I promise you that."

"What if it's too late? He's stabbed three people and two of them are dead."

"If he wanted to kill her, her body would've been there with her car. Instead, he took both. That means she's alive somewhere, and he's got something else planned for her."

"But what?" The pounding of his heart was deafening in his own ears and his hands were shaking. "What could he possibly be planning?"

"He's going to burn another building down."

"I'm sure he will."

"And she'll be in it."

A chill passed over Landon Fox unlike anything he'd ever experienced before. He loved Jerrica with all his heart, and the one thing he hated more than anything was the thing that would take her away from him, if Bob was right. He couldn't let that happen. There were only two more locations, and one of them had to be it. But which one? How would they know?

"What do I do?" he heard himself say over the buzzing in his ears.

"Nothing. You let us handle it. We'll take care of it and we'll find her, Landon. Trust us."

"I don't trust anybody except me to bring her home, and I *will* bring her home." Landon was surprised at how strong his voice was. It wasn't wishful thinking. He had every intention of living up to that pronouncement.

He'd find Jerrica and bring her home. They'd have a long, happy life together. What would happen after that he didn't know and he didn't care. He only knew he couldn't live without her. And he was about to prove it by saving her life.

* * *

By the time he got to the firehouse, deputies were already there, conferring with the captain and making plans. Two FBI agents had already shown up, and Bob was due to make an appearance at any time. Landon was trying to be optimistic, but it was getting harder and harder.

Two hours later, he was still sitting there, wanting to go out and look but being told to sit still. Two turned to three, and at the four-hour mark, he felt crazed, his mind taking him all kinds of places he didn't want it to go.

The police patrolled all night, watching the two buildings, but there was no sign of anything wrong at either location. Where were they? What was happening? Was she okay? Landon felt helpless and small, watching the clock tick away while Jerrica was only god knew where.

But at eight fifteen the next morning, he had an epiphany. While everyone else was on phones and talking together, he slipped out the back and started walking. He walked the entire nine blocks to the courthouse and scaled the steps, then made his way directly to the county clerk's office. "Geneva," he said when he stepped into the room, "have you had anybody in here asking about land titles?"

"Sure did. Couple of guys. Said they were looking to buy some property and wanted to know who it belonged to," the old clerk told him. Geneva had been a member of his parents' church all his life, and he'd grown up with her grandkids. Dirt was old; Geneva was older.

"Did they by any chance ask to see any blueprints that were on file too?"

"Matter of fact, they did."

"Do you remember what they were?"

"Of course I do, sweetie! They were for the church, the library branch, and the daycare center. I'm not sure why, but they asked me to make a copy of the plans for the library so they could take the copy with them, so I made a copy."

"Can I see those plans?"

"Sure! Let me get 'em. I hear you got a lady friend. Boy, it's long past time for that for you!"

"Thanks." *Just get the damn plans,* he wanted to scream, but he kept himself in check.

"Here ya go. I can make you a copy too if you want."

"No. That's okay. Do you remember them asking you anything about the blueprints?"

"Nope, but they were really interested in them." She handed him the roll and walked away.

Landon took the blueprints to a nearby table and rolled them out. Poring over them, he saw nothing that would give him any indication which property the arsonist might target next. The library was three floors, two and a basement, but there was one thing that probably made it appealing.

It was full of papers. Books, documents, and if he remembered correctly, that was the branch where they kept all the reference materials and genealogical information. The basement had tall, tall shelving units full of extremely large, heavy volumes. Many were census reports, some were history books, but they were all lengthy tomes, or at least most of them were. Plenty of fuel. Of course, he knew something else the arsonists probably weren't counting on.

Books are hard to burn. Their compactness and the tightness of their pages mean a higher temperature has to be reached to burn them. It's why many families keep family documents in bibles. It's why the author Ray Bradbury's *Fahrenheit 451* has become mandatory reading over the years in a lot of college classes. Landon thought about that and wondered: On what level would the arsonist build the fire? If he'd taken Jerrica, the guy thought he had something to prove. Starting the fire in the basement wouldn't be showy enough. He'd probably go to one of the upper levels, and that could help.

Landon didn't walk—he ran back to the firehouse. "Captain, I need to talk to you."

"We need to talk to you too, Fox. This is someone you haven't met but you already know."

"Landon, Bob Clark. I'm here to help however I can, and I've got about a dozen agents coming in."

"Thank you. We can use the help. Captain, I really believe this guy is going to hit the library."

"Because of the combustibles?"

"Yes, sir, and because he can make a big show of it."

"I've been thinking that too. Law enforcement needs to be prepared."

"We'll do everything we can," Bob said.

"Thanks." Landon was growing frantic. It obviously

wasn't a kidnapping for ransom—no call had been received and she'd been gone almost twenty-four hours. This was something different, something sinister, and he was terrified.

Skeeter came running into the office and skidded to a stop. "Captain Martin! The sergeant wants to talk to you!"

"Better see what he wants." Landon followed the captain until he reached the police sergeant. "Yes, sir. What can I do for you?"

"We just received this." The man handed a zippered evidence bag to the captain. He took it and turned it over. Inside was a scrawled note, but it was easy to read.

Even little kids won't stop me. It's coming down.

"Well, now we know where to put our resources," Captain Martin murmured.

"No, sir! Don't you see? He's trying to divert us! It's the library, I know it is!" Landon almost screamed.

"Lieutenant, this is pretty clear. We'll direct our resources toward the daycare center and hope we're right."

"Sir, please, he knows what he's doing. This isn't ..."

"Lieutenant, I have to agree with your captain," the police sergeant said. "This is the only indication we have of what he might do. We've got to go with it."

"But sir—"

"My decision is final, Fox," Captain Martin snapped.

"You and your men will be on standby awaiting further instructions. Carry on."

Landon stepped out of the captain's office feeling as defeated as he ever had. A hand on his shoulder turned him and he found Bob standing there. "For what it's worth, I think you're right, but my superiors are going to tell us to follow the evidence trail, so my hands are tied."

"Of course they are. Nobody will help me. Guess I'm on my own with this. But if she dies, so help me god—"

"Don't think like that. Try to be positive. She's got a strong will to live because of you. You're going to come through this, Landon. I just know it."

"God, I hope you're right," Landon mumbled. "I really, really hope you're right."

CHAPTER 9

Jerrica's hands were cramping behind her back, and the pain was almost unbearable. She was thirsty too, and she'd peed her pants, but there was nothing she could do about it except wait. Landon would come for her. She was sure of it.

"Can't I please just have some water?" she whined, hoping the guy was out there, but only silence greeted her. *How long have I been here?* she wondered. It had been late afternoon when he took her from the parking lot. How was Stan? She was sure the guy had attacked him. Stan was divorced and had three kids. It was important for their father to be in their lives. Was he okay? She felt terrible that her situation had put him in danger.

It was quiet, so quiet, and she wondered if that space, whatever it was, would become her tomb. Would they even find her body? The air around her was musty with the smell of old linens and urine, the latter being her own. Maybe a hotel room? Maybe a closet somewhere? She wasn't sure.

All she knew was that she had to fight the demons raging in her head, the ones telling her that her life was over, and fight to be with Landon. He was all that mattered.

* * *

"No! Stop! Get your hands off me!" Jerrica screamed, and the guy hit her hard enough to knock her down.

"Get up and shut up, stupid bitch! We're going for a walk, and you'd better be quiet. I don't have time for this shit. Let's go."

"Could I *please* just have a drink of water? Please?"

"No water. No nothing. You pissed your damn pants, and I don't need that mess in my car. Jesus, grow the fuck up and shut up!" the voice hissed at her as he grabbed her roughly by her bound arms and dragged her, backward, from wherever she'd been and away.

"Where are we going?" she asked.

"What does it matter? You're not going anywhere I don't take you, so you don't have a say anyway."

"My boyfriend's looking for me, you know. He'll find me and when he does, he'll kill you," she spat through the black hood he'd kept over her face.

"Yeah, yeah. He's not going to catch me. That's the

thing. So, honestly, I'm not worried about that one little bit."

Cool night air hit the skin on her wrists where the rope bit in and Jerrica knew they were outside. "Where are we?"

"God. I hate to have to do this because I wanted to hear you scream, but you've left me no choice." She had no idea what he was talking about until something pressed into her face and she smelled that same odor from earlier.

And she was out.

* * *

Bob had told Landon there were agents stationed everywhere around the daycare. If he was coming there, he'd be caught, and he'd sure as hell never get Jerrica inside.

It didn't matter. They shouldn't be going there—Landon was growing more positive of that by the hour. No amount of talking, of begging and pleading, had gotten anybody to listen to him, and they were all focused on the daycare center, a small, one-story building with an all-glass front. It was absurd to think that would be his target if he'd gone to the trouble to snatch Jerrica, and yet that was their focus, as wrong as he thought they were.

He sat in the firehouse and waited, bouncing his heel on the floor. It had been almost thirty-six hours since she'd first gone missing. It was the wee hours of the morning, and nothing was stirring outside. If anyone was moving around, the agents at the daycare center would certainly see them.

But the sun rose and nothing happened. Landon stared at the clock. Forty hours. She'd been gone forty hours and nothing. She had to be terrified out of her mind, and that broke Landon's heart. Jerrica was depending on him to find her, and he was doing nothing. He couldn't just sit there, but he couldn't figure out what to do.

At noon, the FBI agents pulled out and went into stand-down mode. There were a couple of calls, a brush fire at a farm right inside the city limits and an elderly man whose walker was stuck in a doorway and he was trapped. Landon hadn't slept in almost three days. He told the guys he'd be no good to them and to go without him.

Late evening sunlight was fading as he stood in the doorway of the firehouse and looked up and down the street. It was quiet, a typical evening in Taylorsville. The downtown offices, what there were of them, were closed, and nobody was going to the post office across the street. The occasional deputy and police officer cruised by and waved at him, but he felt like the whole world had given up. Jerrica was out there somewhere, and no one was looking. Oh, he knew Bob and his crew were sifting through information, running the note they'd received through handwriting analysis, but none of that was going to help. By the time they found her, she'd be dead, and he would want to die too. Without her, life had no meaning anymore.

The guys sat around the station house's kitchen table playing poker quietly. Occasionally one would ask, "Hey, Hose, don't you wanna play?"

"No thanks." He couldn't play a fucking game while she was out there somewhere. It couldn't happen. He'd had to deal with her parents earlier in the afternoon, tell them what was happening, and it had been total hell listening to her mother cry and beg him to find her daughter. Didn't she know there was nothing else on his mind? That he was paralyzed until she was back in his arms? Didn't anyone realize his world was ending and he was powerless to stop it?

And then, at eleven seventeen that evening, all hell broke loose.

"Station Two, Station Two, report of smoke coming from the Taylorsville Public Library's downtown branch, two oh nine West Main Street. Repeat, smoke sited at the Taylorsville Public Library's downtown branch, two oh—"

"Jesus Christ!" Landon screamed into the void of the station house. "I tried to tell *all* of you! Get your asses in these trucks and LET'S ROLL!"

To their credit, he'd never seen his men move so fast in their lives. They were ready to tear out when Captain Martin appeared in full turnout gear. "Believe me now?" Landon spat at him.

"Following leads, firefighter. You can argue with me or we can roll." As soon as the captain was on board, Landon signaled Red and the truck raced out of the bay.

That truck couldn't move fast enough. By the time they got there, two black FBI Suburbans were parked nearby and Agent Clark ran toward the firefighters. "We got here as soon as we could. Haven't seen any sign of anyone around, but that doesn't mean much."

"Thanks, but you need to move back. We've got a fire to fight," Landon told him as politely as he could muster. It was up to him to find her and save her, and he didn't know what that would entail.

It didn't matter. He'd bring her back even if it killed him, and there was a distinct possibility that it might.

Smoke poured from the upstairs windows. Two stories and a basement, as he recalled from the blueprints. It had been years since he'd been in the building, but he remembered a few details. One was that it had been an old house, and the other was the pride people in the town and the library system took in talking about the structure of the house. Of particular interest were the stairs. They were one long set with landings on the various floors, and were made with wooden pegs. Landon knew what that meant. If the pegs burned, the stairs would completely fall apart, and it didn't matter which level burned. The whole structure of the stairs depended on its entirety, and any missing section spelled doom. Even worse was the fact that, due to its age, a fire suppression system hadn't been a requirement. They'd all regret that, he was sure.

On top of all the other disastrous components, the basement had tiny windows. No one could get in or out of them, regardless if they were broken. He stood there, wondering if the maniac had put her on the second floor and used accelerant to start the fire. Was she already dead? Trucks were coming in from everywhere in anticipation of a huge fire, but Landon knew it would smolder for days once the initial loose materials burned. Problem was, the weight of the books and shelves would aid in the collapse, and adding water would make that danger worse. But without water, the whole thing would go up.

He tried to think like an arsonist, but he couldn't. How could he do that? Nothing they did made sense to him, and yet he understood why these fires had been set. Someone yelled, "Power's off!" That was courtesy of the electric company truck that had shown up, and only the battery-powered security lights inside glowed. They were free to pour it on, but at that point, only the upstairs windows were accessible.

Landon couldn't wait another minute. He ran back to the truck and grabbed a respirator. "What are you doing?" Captain Martin yelled.

"I'm going in."

"No. You're not. Stand down, firefighter."

Landon wheeled on his superior. "I'm not standing down! Jerrica's in there somewhere, and—"

"You don't know that!"

"Like I didn't know it would be the library? I'm sorry, sir, but this is one time I'm going to have to ignore your command. I'm going in that building, so get the hell out of my way." Strapping his respirator on, he glanced around. "Somebody give me theirs?"

"You can have mine," Red answered and handed his mask and tank to Landon.

"Thanks, man. See you on the other side." Toting the extra respirator and the biggest fire blanket they had on the truck, Landon took off at a dead run for the side door of the library. He knew it opened right onto the staircase, and it was his best bet to access the building.

"Fox, get back here! That's an order!" Captain Martin shouted.

Landon spun and ran backward. "Sir, I quit." With that, he sprinted for the door and shoved a shoulder into it to knock it in.

Blackness consumed him. Smoke was everywhere, but the first floor wasn't in flames yet, just saturated with the swirling tendrils. He marched into the main area around the circulation desk and watched as ceiling tiles turned black from the heat above. "Jerrica! Jerrica, are you in here?" he screamed, but she didn't answer. Trying the stairs, he realized he couldn't go up to the second floor. Wallpaper curled as flames licked up the walls, and if she was up there, it was too late. There was one more area he could check, and he headed back down the stairs, listening to the hiss and pop of the flames above and the creaking of the treads as he climbed downward.

"Jerrica? Jerrica, are you down here? Baby, it's me! It's Landon! If you're here, please, let me know!" Silence met his ears. All he could hear was the sound of crackling and popping above.

And then he heard it. "Landon?"

"Jerrica! Baby, where are you? Keep talking, babe! I'm looking for you!"

"I don't know! It's too dark! I don't know where I am!"

"Station Two, we're in the basement. Repeat—we're in the basement. Copy?"

"Copy that, Hose," a voice answered, ringing in his ears through his headset.

Landon ran here and there in the stacks, looking up and down aisles. He wasn't sure how many he'd scanned before he found her, wrists tied behind her back and a black pillowcase-like thing over her head. "Baby! I'm here! I'm here! It's gonna be okay!"

"Oh, Landon, I'm so scared! So much smoke!" she cried as he worked to remove the rope from her wrists.

"It's okay. We're going to be fine, I promise. Come on." Yanking the bag off her head, he watched as she looked around while he fitted the extra respirator to her face.

"We're in the library. You were right all along."

"No time for that. We've got to get out of—"

There was a shudder and a groan, and Landon's worst fear came to life. The staircase collapsed, its pieces tumbling down into the basement like large building blocks. It lay in a heap, the top portion smoldering, twisted and piled up until it would be impossible to reach the door. Besides, it was ten feet up. There was no way to climb out.

Think, Fox! a voice yelled in his head. "Get on the floor! Right now!" He waited as Jerrica lay down between some of the shelves and flattened herself on the tile floor. The shelving units would hopefully catch the floors above as they fell, but they'd be trapped between them. Landon lay down on top of her and pulled the fire blanket over them, then thought of something.

He raked books off the shelves as fast as he could, covering the fire blanket with them. They'd burn slowly, so maybe they'd act as a little more insulation from the flames and heat. But he didn't have much hope. There was no other way into the basement other than the side door and the stairs, and neither were usable anymore.

Landon lay down on top of Jerrica and wrapped his arms around her. "Can you breathe, baby?"

"You're heavy!" she said with a laugh, and Landon just hugged her tighter. Saving her was all that mattered, and his body would be a better shield for her than the blanket and books. He'd sacrifice himself willingly if there was any way his fellow firefighters could get her out.

Time stood still as the small space filled with dense, acrid smoke. Jerrica wrapped her arms around his neck and squeezed, and his eyes filled with tears. Their tomorrows would never come. He'd never get the chance to hold a baby they'd made together, or see their first grader play softball. There'd be no wedding ceremony, no anniversary dinners. None of that would happen, but he'd go to his grave with the memories of the time they'd had together. He just hoped when the moment arrived she wasn't too scared. Being terrified wasn't something he wanted her to experience, and he prayed he'd have the good sense to rip the respirator from her face so smoke inhalation would take her before the fire consumed them. The idea that she'd suffer was something he couldn't tolerate.

Time stood still. It was just the two of them with the fire raging, snapping, and popping above them as they lay there, trapped there in that dark, smoky hell. "It's gonna be okay, baby. Don't worry. They'll get to us in time," he whispered down to her.

"What if they don't, Landon? What if they can't?"

"My guys won't let me down." *God, I hope I'm not lying to her,* he told himself as he gave her another squeeze. Then another sound filled his ears.

Tick. Tick. Tick. Plop. Tick. Plop.

"Do you hear that?" he asked her.

"What?"

"Listen." Now it was faster, the sounds closer

together, and it was coming from more than one direction. "Hear it?"

"What is that?"

Tears stung Landon's eyes. "It's water. They've broken through the roof. It won't take long to put out the flames once they get enough water on it." But he knew the awful truth.

The addition of the water would make the upper floors heavy, so heavy that the old wood wouldn't be able to hold them. There was no way they'd get out of there. It was as good as over.

There was a rumble and the floor trembled beneath them. He immediately knew what that meant—the building was giving way. They'd be buried in smoldering floor joists in a matter of seconds, and he gripped the most precious thing he'd ever held just a little tighter.

But in an instant, everything changed when Landon saw beams of light from under the edge of the blanket. Peering out just a little, he realized the basement was completely illuminated, a brilliant white light pouring in. "Fox! Lieutenant Fox! Are you here?"

"Over here! Come on, baby, get up!" When he'd knocked all the books and the blanket off and helped her stand, he was flabbergasted.

A huge, gaping hole in the concrete basement wall filled his vision, and two large pieces of earth-moving equipment stood just outside the perimeter. "Louisville

Search and Rescue! We've got to get you guys out of here! Come on!" a rescue worker yelled as he grabbed Jerrica by the arm and pulled her along. Another pulled Landon with him, and together the four scrambled out of the hole in the side of the basement foundation and into the light of the Disaster and Emergency Services emergency lighting rigs. They ran as fast as they could to get clear of the building. From behind them came a mighty shudder and the interior floors of the old library collapsed, sending ash and sparks forty feet into the air.

"You okay?" one of the men asked Landon when they were about two hundred feet away.

"Don't worry about me. Worry about her. She's my only concern. Please, just check on her," he barked and pointed as Jerrica's respirator was removed and she choked and coughed.

"We've got a bus out front waiting to take both of you to the hospital. Let's get you loaded up." The two rescue workers accompanied them to the front of the building, and when they rounded the corner, Landon got a big surprise.

Every firefighter in the area began to cheer. His guys were slapping him on the back, tousling his hair, and grabbing his hands as he walked by. By the time they made it to the bus, Red and Stingray were there, taking their respirators and Landon's turnout gear so he wouldn't have to carry it back from the hospital. In seconds, they were strapped onto gurneys and hurtling through the city streets toward the very hospital where Jerrica spent her days helping others.

"Jerrica! Oh my god! Are you okay?" Brandy screamed as they rolled the firefighter and the nurse in.

"I'm okay! Landon saved me!" she shouted back as the gurney kept rolling.

Two hours later, it was determined they were fine, with just some irritation of the linings of their lungs. Nothing more serious. They lay in the emergency room cubicle, gurneys side by side, their hands entwined, and Landon brushed her knuckles with his thumb. "Baby," he whispered, "I'm so sorry."

Jerrica looked at him like he'd lost his mind. "For what?"

Shame washed over him and he knew his cheeks were crimson. "I told you I'd protect you and I didn't."

"Landon Fox! You saved my life!"

"I let him take you."

"You didn't *let* him do anything! He stabbed Stan, for god's sake! By the way, I need to find out how he's doing."

That was the moment the curtain opened and Landon groaned. "Oh, god, not you."

"Calm down, big brother. Just hang on. Can we talk for a second?"

"About how stupid I am? Because if that's what you've—"

"No! Stop! I'm thankful you're alive! Jesus, Mom and Dad are having a come-apart, and poor Liella is beside herself worrying about both of you." Brandon sat down on the foot of Landon's gurney, and the older twin waited, steeling himself for what he was sure was coming. "Look, I don't understand why you love firefighting so much. God knows it's a dangerous occupation. But …" Brandon took a deep breath. "You're not going to get any more shit from me. I wouldn't have been brave enough to do what you did tonight to save Maria. I know I couldn't. But you didn't hesitate. I respect that. I respect you. I know you've worked hard to get where you are, and I respect that too. I don't know if Mom and Dad will ever accept it, but I think I understand a little better now why you do what you do, and I'm grateful there are men like you in our community who are willing to put themselves out there."

Landon could feel his eyes bugging. "Who are you and what have you done with my brother?"

Brandon laughed. "It's me, I swear. I'm thankful you're okay and this little lady will be okay too," he said and patted Jerrica's hand. She looked at Landon, her eyes wide, and shrugged. "You just need to go home and get some rest. I'm going out to ask Dr. Reed to sign your discharge papers and I'll drive the two of you home."

Jerrica interrupted. "I want to stop by my parents' house."

"We can do that too," Brandon assured her. "Not a problem. Let's get you ready to go."

* * *

A shower. That was what he needed more than anything. That and clean clothes. Everything smelled like smoke—everything. He even left his boots outside the back door because he couldn't stand the stench. Jerrica was mad because she'd been wearing her favorite scrubs and athletic shoes, and he'd finally convinced her that they couldn't be salvaged, but not before she had a fit.

Landon was making sure all the doors were locked and the alarm set when his phone rang. "Who in the world is calling me at four thirty in the morning?" he asked himself, but he was shocked when he saw that it was Agent Clark's number. "Hello?"

"Landon? I didn't wake you, did I?"

"No. We just got showered and ready for bed. What's up?"

"We got your arsonist!"

"What? When? Where? Are you serious?"

"Yeah. One of our agents was looking around and saw drag marks in the alley behind the library. Turns out he's been holed up in a rental house over here this whole time. KMM Holdings had already bought it with the intention of destroying it. It would've been the last property he burned if we hadn't caught him."

"He was right there the whole time." Landon couldn't believe it.

"Yep. So that's finished. He'll be charged with two

counts of murder and one count of attempted homicide for the security guard, and kidnapping, holding against her will, terroristic threatening, and attempted murder for what he did to Jerrica. Tomorrow they're carrying out a raid of KMM Holdings' offices and we expect more arrests. But if you hadn't put the pieces together, we might not have any of this, so thank you, Lieutenant Fox."

"Thank you, Bob. I appreciate everything the bureau did, and when you talk to Agent Livingston, could you tell him that for me too, please? For both of us?"

"I'll do it. Take care. I'm sure I'll see you in the next couple of days as we're wrapping things up."

"Great. See you later. Bye." Landon stood there, still trying to process the information. When he reached the bedroom, he grinned. "They caught the guy."

"Seriously? I don't have to be afraid anymore? Where did they catch him?"

"They saw drag marks in the alley where he dragged you from the house behind the library."

"I was in the house behind the library? I had no idea! Wow. He's gone and it's over," Jerrica said almost reverently.

"Yeah. And I'm glad they gave you fluids at the hospital. Babe, you were horribly dehydrated."

"And I smelled like pee. Don't forget that."

"It's already forgotten, sweetheart," Landon said

with a chuckle. "But what I said about not protecting you—"

"Shush it, Landon Fox. Things happen in this world that nobody anticipates. You did everything you could to keep me safe. Everybody did. In the end, you saved my life. That's all that matters." Taking his hand and turning it palm up, Jerrica pulled it to her face and kissed his fingertips one by one. Landon's eyes filled with tears. God, he loved that woman! She was the best thing in his life, and he had no intention of letting anything happen to her ever again.

"Baby, I want to marry you as soon as I can. Please? If you want the white dress and fancy invitations and all that, it's fine, but I really—"

"I don't need any of that." Palms pressed to his cheeks, she tipped his head until she could stare straight into his eyes. "All I really want or need is you. I'm ready for our forever."

"I'm ready for our forever too." With a finger under her chin, he tipped her head back and pressed his lips to her soft, warm ones. Everything in his world, all the ragged edges and ripped corners, smoothed in that moment as the rest of the world melted away and it was only the two of them, there in that room where they made love night after night.

Life was precious. That point had been driven home in the most painful of ways. The tomorrows Landon thought they'd lost were stretched out before them like a golden road into the future, and he knew they'd walk it hand in hand. He wanted to look into her eyes as she said "I do," watch her belly grow round and taut with their child, see the wrinkles etch into her face and watch her hair turn white. He wanted it all. And he'd have it with her.

Their forever started in that moment, and he couldn't have been more ready.

* * *

Two days. That was all the time he felt he could take before he had to face the captain, and he'd made his peace with what he had to say. He didn't have to wait long. As soon as he walked into the station house that day, he heard Captain Martin yell, "Fox!"

"Good luck, bro," Stingray said and slapped his shoulder.

"Stand your ground, man," Tinman warned.

"Thanks, guys." Landon made his way down the hallway and stood in the doorway. "Yes, sir."

"Come in, close the door, and take a seat." Landon did as the captain said and sat down in the chair directly in front of his desk. "We need to have a talk."

"Yes, sir."

"Fox, I gave you a direct order to stand down and you disobeyed my command."

"Yes, sir."

"You do realize that is grounds for dismissal."

"Yes, sir, but I told you I quit. I came in today to turn in my badge."

The captain's forearms left the surface of his desk and he reared back in the big desk chair. "I told you to stand down for a reason. The building was unstable. We hadn't had time to assess it. Thankfully, the power had already been shut off when you went running in there, but you threw caution to the wind and ignored everything you've ever been taught."

"Yes, sir." It was true, all of it, and there was no reason to deny it.

"I'd be well within my rights to dismiss you right now." The captain stood, walked around the desk, and sat down on the front edge, his knees almost touching Landon's. "But I also know we're always in need of people who'll think outside the box. Moreover, we need people who have good instincts and know how to use them. That could've been a tragedy, firefighter. Instead, you saved a life. For that, you should be commended. You exemplify everything we promote in the department, despite the fact that you ignored a command. You knew something more important—you knew when to ignore your commanding officer and go with your gut. Your men admire and follow you, and you set a great example for them in bravery and tenacity. You inspire them to go above and beyond the call of duty, and we need more leadership like that." Landon couldn't believe what he was hearing. The captain was *commending* him? He thought he couldn't possibly be more surprised.

But he was wrong. "This isn't common knowledge, so I'd appreciate it if you'd keep it to yourself. But Ezra Murphy is retiring in six months as battalion chief, and they've asked me to take the position."

"Congratulations, sir."

"Thank you. And I'm recommending you be made captain of Station Two."

"Wha-what? Sir?"

"You heard me. I think you'd make a great captain, and I'm also recommending that Red take the lieutenant's position once you're promoted. He's earned it."

"Ye-ye-yes, sir. Thank you, sir. I mean, wow. Thanks. I . . . What can I say?"

"Say, 'I'm sorry, captain, and I won't do that again.'"

Landon snorted and shook his head. "I'm sorry, captain, but I can't do that. If the circumstances were similar, I'd do the same thing all over again."

Captain Martin sighed. "I know. Hence the advancement recommendation. Fox, go home. Take a couple more days off. And do us all a favor."

"Yes, sir?"

"Marry that girl before you come back to work. The two of you belong together more than any two people I've ever seen. I'm thankful you got her back and she's okay. Now get the hell out of here before I change my mind and yank your badge," Captain Martin said with a grin.

"Yes, sir!" Landon strode out of the office and back up the hallway.

"Ready to go back to work?" Stingray asked.

"Nope. Going home to my girl. I'll be back in a couple of days. And congratulate me."

Bobo stared at him. "Why?"

"I'm getting married!"

* * *

Her parents. Her brother and sister-in-law. His parents. His brother and sister-in-law. His sister. That was it. Nobody else. They stood in front of the judge the next day and made it official. They were Mr. and Mrs. Landon Fox.

After the ceremony, they went straight to The Blue Moon and Landon bought drinks for all their friends. All the nurses from the hospital were there, all the guys from the station house, and Dr. Reed and Dr. Blankenship even showed up! Everyone laughed and talked and the hours flew. When they got ready to leave, Landon's truck was covered with toilet paper and shaving cream, and they drove straight to his cousin's cabin on Taylorsville Lake for one night alone in the great outdoors.

That night, when her fingers ran over Landon's bare skin, Jerrica knew she was home. No matter where they were, as long as they were together, it would be their home. Their lovemaking was epic, something she couldn't get enough of as his hands roamed her body and caressed every part of her that made her his. When they were finished, she lay with her cheek pressed to his chest, her fingers dawdling through the hair in its center and skimming up and down his happy trail. "There's something I want to ask you."

Landon sighed into her hair. "Okay."

"I want to stop taking my pills." She lifted her head so she could see his expression. Judging from the peaking of his eyebrows, he was totally surprised.

"Yeah?"

"Yeah. How do you feel about that?"

"I feel good about that. But are you sure you're ready?"

"I'm not getting any younger, Landon."

"Neither am I. I'm past ready."

"Good. We'll get to work on baby Fox as soon as the pills get out of my system."

"Sounds good to me. And before all this shit started, did you get that research done?"

"I did. I got the name of the doctor and everything."

"Good. Let's set that in motion. Can't happen too soon."

He was right. It couldn't. They'd found happiness. It was time his sister had some too.

EPILOGUE

Six weeks later

She'd been given the option of two people to be in the room while the procedure was taking place, and that had been tough. Jerrica was a nurse and she'd set it all up, but Liella had chosen her mother and Landon. The doctor came in and smiled down into her face. "Now, we're going to knock you out with propofol. It's not that this is terribly painful, but we can't have you moving around while we're trying to place the needle. It'll only take us about thirty minutes start to finish. I know that's scary for you, to be out of control, but your brother and your mother are here."

"You know we won't let anything happen to you," Louella told her daughter.

Liella had begun to cry. "I know, but I'm scared! What if it doesn't work?"

The doctor patted her arm. "We've had great

success with the stellate ganglion blocks. I think with that and cognitive behavior therapy, you'll see a lot of improvement in a very short time. So are you okay to move forward?" Liella nodded. "They're going to put the medication into your IV and you'll be fine. Just count backward from one hundred."

One hundred. Ninety-nine, ninety-eight, ninety-seven, ninety ...

Her eyelids fluttered and she glanced around. "How long have I been out?"

"About twenty-five minutes. We're all finished! But you'll have to stay for about an hour so we can monitor you. We've got a very comfortable room for you down the hall, if you'd like to go now," the nurse told her.

"Yes, please." As the gurney rolled down the hallway, Landon took her hand and held it, walking along beside her. The room was pretty, and the sun shone in the big windows that looked out over a courtyard between wings of the building.

"Try to take a little nap and I'll be back in a bit," the nurse offered as she left the room. Liella closed her eyes. She didn't *feel* different, but how would she know?

When she woke again, she looked at the clock. She'd been asleep for about forty minutes. Landon was in a chair across the room, eyes closed and breathing quietly. Louella was reading a magazine, and she looked up. "Hi, honey! How do you feel?"

"Okay, I guess." Liella sat up and dangled her legs off the side of the bed. "Did I bring any slippers?"

"No, I don't think so. These floors are clean, so don't worry about it. Do you need to go to the bathroom?"

"Yeah. I do."

"Need some help?"

"No. I think I can do it." She stood and headed across the room to the bathroom. When she reached it, she closed the door. And she realized something important.

She almost never closed the bathroom door. She was afraid to be alone in there, where no one could see her. Public restrooms were horrible because of the stalls. And yet she'd closed the door when she walked in without even thinking about it. When she was finished, she washed her hands, dried them, and headed back to the gurney.

"I need to dress," she told her mother.

"Landon, let's go out in the hallway so Liella can get dressed." A drowsy Landon rose and followed Louella out, and Liella went about putting all her clothes back on, including her shoes and socks.

There was a tap on the door. "Come in." Instead of her mother or Landon, a young man in scrubs stood there. "Oh! Do you have the wrong room?"

"Are you Liella Fox?"

"Yes, sir."

"Dr. Colby wants to see you in his office down the hall. Will you come with me, please?"

"Uh, okay." She let the young man hold the door for her. When she stepped out into the hallway, her mother and Landon were nowhere to be found.

"This way," he told her and wandered down the hallway, speaking to nurses as he passed them. When he reached the end, he opened a door.

Dr. Colby, Landon, and Louella sat in chairs in the office. "Liella!" Dr. Colby called out brightly. "Come and have a seat."

She sat and watched the three others in the room turn and smile at her. "What?"

"Honey," Louella asked, tears in her eyes, "do you realize you just followed a stranger down a hallway and never blinked?"

The realization hit her between the eyes like a mallet. "Oh my god. I wasn't scared of him."

"No. You weren't. Tell me, if Landon invited you to go to a bar with him tonight to meet some friends, do you think you'd go?" Dr. Colby asked.

Her gaze passed to Landon and she smiled, tears rolling down her face. "Yes. I think I would, as long as he was going to be there."

Dr. Colby rounded the desk and sat down on the edge in front of Liella. "This is your new reality. You need to be attending cognitive behavior therapy appointments, but I'd say most of your progress has just been made. Go enjoy your life. I'll see you back here in six weeks to make sure things are going okay. You can make an appointment at the desk on your way out. And thank you for trusting me with your care. I want you to keep a diary so you can tell me about all the things you've done when you come back, okay?"

"Yes, sir. I'll do it. Thank you." Liella looked at her hands. Over the last few years, they'd looked weird and foreign to her, but now they just looked like hands. Her hands. Things looked completely different, but in a good way.

For the first time in a long time, she walked out of the medical building into the sunlight and wasn't afraid of the people walking around on the sidewalks and in the parking lot. She rode in the back seat of the car and when the man in traffic beside them turned and looked at her, she smiled at him. To her astonishment, he smiled back.

She'd been terrified on the flight to Los Angeles because of all the people. They'd fly back the next morning, and she had a feeling she was going to enjoy it immensely.

* * *

Eight and a half months later

"Oh, look how cute!" Jerrica squealed as she held up the little romper. "Thank you, Brandy!"

"And what's this?" Mina asked as they pushed a huge package into the room.

Jerrica ripped the paper off the back. "Oh my god! It's our crib! Who did this?"

Louella raised her hand. "Robert and I wanted you to have it. He knew you and Landon had picked it out, and it was the nicest thing we could buy for you, so we got it. I hope it's what you wanted."

"Yes! Oh, god, it's so beautiful! Thank you!" Jerrica struggled to her feet and waddled toward her mother-in-law, leaned down and kissed the older woman, then straightened and called out, "Landon! Come in here and look! It's the crib!"

He appeared in the doorway from the den where he was hanging out with all the guys. "Oh, wow! That's awesome, baby!"

"Isn't it?"

"Okay, guys, it's time," Liella announced. They'd put her in charge of the shower, and she'd had a great time pulling it together. Betsy and Jolie had helped her, but there was one part she hadn't let anyone help with.

Landon and Jerrica had handed her the unopened envelope with the baby's sex. They didn't even know what it was. They'd also given her the names they'd chosen for a boy and a girl. She'd had a banner made, and it draped across the room above the table where the cake and punch sat, rolled up with a ripcord on either end. When they pulled the cord, the banner would unfurl downward and it would welcome the new baby with whatever name was appropriate for its sex. She'd never seen a gender reveal like that, and she couldn't wait to see their faces.

"Oh, my god, I'm so nervous," Jerrica whispered to Landon loudly enough that everybody could hear, and they all laughed.

Landon bellowed, "Guys! Get out here! It's the moment everybody's been waiting for!" They'd asked Station Four to cover for them, so every firefighter from the station house, including Battalion Chief Martin and Elise, was there.

"Pull the damn cord already. The suspense is killing us!" Rodeo barked.

Landon grinned. "Okay. On the count of three. One, two, THREE!" Landon and Jerrica yanked the cords and the banner unrolled to applause.

Welcome, Landon Simpson Fox, Jr.!

Landon grabbed Jerrica and lifted her off her feet, spinning her and kissing her as everyone laughed and clapped. Liella was so proud. She'd pulled it off! It had gone great and everyone was over-the-moon happy.

As soon as everyone had been served cake and drinks, she excused herself to go down the hallway to the bathroom. She was almost to the door when a huge figure with copper-colored hair ran headlong into her. "Oh!"

"Oh, god, sorry," Red mumbled. "I didn't see you there. Are you okay?"

"Yeah, yeah. You just startled me, that's all."

"I'm so sorry. I didn't mean to. Sure you're okay?"

"Yeah. I'm fine. Red, right?"

He grinned. "Yep. Well, better get back to the party. Watch out in dark hallways, okay?" he said with a laugh.

"I'll take that under advisement!" she replied with a giggle.

Two hours later, she was standing in the kitchen scraping cake off plates when Jerrica appeared at her side. "Liella, thank you soooo much. This was too much fun, and you did an awesome job."

"Thanks. Hey, Jerr?"

"Yeah?"

She bowed her head a little to hide her smile. "I've been thinking that I might like to, you know, get into circulation."

"Get into ... Oh! Get into circulation? Really?"

"Yeah. You know, give it a whirl."

"Well, I happen to know for a fact that you have an admirer," Jerrica whispered to her.

"I do?"

"Yep."

"Who?"

"You probably daydream about a tall, muscled-up brunette or a blond, right?" Liella nodded. "Well, what about a ginger?" Without another word, she waddled out of the room.

A ginger. Liella smiled. Yeah, a ginger would do nicely.

Yes—Liella is going to get her own story! Book 8 in the Bluegrass Bravery series will be hers. You'll hear from a lot of the characters in this book when you read that one. Happy reading!

NOTE: The SGB (stellate ganglion block) was used for years for pain relief, but clinical studies have shown it is extremely effective on PTSD, especially cases which have been resistant to other traditional therapies, and often is far cheaper. Simple and effective, it consists of applying a small amount of an anesthetic agent to the stellate ganglion, which in effect reboots the "fight or flight" instinct within the brain, much as rebooting a computer. Sometimes, but rarely, two treatments are required. It can work in as little as thirty minutes, and its effects can last for years. Simply doing a search online for "stellate ganglion block PTSD" will give anyone all the information they require regarding treatment, costs, and where to find a clinician. It's my fervent hope that someday this treatment will be available to anyone and everyone who needs it.

ABOUT THE AUTHOR ...

Deanndra Hall is a working author living in the far western end of the beautiful Bluegrass State with her husband of over 35 years and small menagerie of weird little dogs. When she's not writing, she's editing. When she's doing neither of those two things, she's having dinner with friends, spending time with family, kayaking, eating chocolate, drinking beer or moonshine, or looking for something that she put in the wrong place and can't seem to find (which is pretty much everything she owns).

On the Web: www.deanndrahall.com

Email: Deanndra@deanndrahall.com

Facebook: facebook.com/deanndra.hall

Instagram: deanndra_hall

Twitter: twitter.com/DeanndraHall

Goodreads: goodreads.com/DeanndraHall
Bookbub: bookbub.com/authors/deanndra-hall

Stay in touch. For all the latest news, contests, exclusive content and more sign up for my newsletter: www.subscribepage.com/deanndrahall

ALSO BY DEANNDRA HALL

* * *

Bluegrass Bravery

Shelter for Sharla

Justice for Aleta

Shelter for Martina

Justice for Daesha

Shelter for Jerrica

Tarpley VFD Series

Fighting for Carly

The Love Under Construction Series

Laying a Foundation with prequel, The Groundbreaking

Tearing Down Walls

Renovating a Heart

Planning an Addition

The Citadel Series

One Simple Mistake

One Broken Promise

One Poor Choice

One Wrong Glance

The Legacy Series

Atonement

Legacy of Freedom

Legacy of Faithfulness

The Witch of Endor Series

Laid Bare

Ripped Open

Torn Apart

The Harper's Cove Series

Karen and Brett at 326 Harper's Cove

Becca and Greg at 314 Harper's Cove

Donna and Connor at 228 Harper's Cove

Savannah and Martin at 219 Harper's Cove

Cheryl and Samuel at 323 Harper's Cove

Tasha and Davis at 333 Harper's Cove

Lily and Brock at 343 Harper's Cove

Siobhán and Gabhain at 241 Harper's Cove

The Me, You, and Us Series

Adventurous Me

Unforgettable You

Incredible Us

The Celtic Fan (independent novel)

Rough Stock (part of the Bad Girls of Romance Series)

The Silent Cove Series

Awakening

Retribution, by Anne L. Parks

Banishing, by Jax Jillian

There are many more books in this fan fiction world than listed here, for an up-to-date list go to www.AcesPress.com

You can also visit our Amazon page at:
http://www.amazon.com/author/operationalpha

Special Forces: Operation Alpha World

Christie Adams: Charity's Heart
Denise Agnew: Dangerous to Hold
Shauna Allen: Awakening Aubrey
Brynne Asher: Blackburn
Linzi Baxter: Unlocking Dreams
Jennifer Becker: Hiding Catherine
Alice Bello: Shadowing Milly
Heather Blair: Rescue Me
Anna Blakely: Rescuing Gracelynn
Amy Briggs: Saving Sarah
Julia Bright: Saving Lorelei
Victoria Bright: Surviving Savage
Cara Carnes: Protecting Mari
Kendra Mei Chailyn: Beast
Melissa Kay Clarke: Rescuing Annabeth
Samantha A. Cole: Handling Haven
Sue Coletta: Hacked
Melissa Combs: Gallant
Anne Conley: Redemption for Misty
KaLyn Cooper: Rescuing Melina
Liz Crowe: Marking Mariah

Sarah Curtis: Securing the Odds
Jordan Dane: Redemption for Avery
Tarina Deaton: Found in the Lost
Aspen Drake, Intense
KL Donn: Unraveling Love
Riley Edwards: Protecting Olivia
PJ Fiala: Defending Sophie
Nicole Flockton: Protecting Maria
Michele Gwynn: Rescuing Emma
Casey Hagen: Shielding Nebraska
Desiree Holt: Protecting Maddie
Kathy Ivan: Saving Sarah
Kris Jacen, Be With Me
Jesse Jacobson: Protecting Honor
Silver James: Rescue Moon
Becca Jameson: Saving Sofia
Kate Kinsley: Protecting Ava
Heather Long: Securing Arizona
Gennita Low: No Protection
Kirsten Lynn: Joining Forces for Jesse
Margaret Madigan: Bang for the Buck
Kimberly McGath: The Predecessor
Rachel McNeely: The SEAL's Surprise Baby
KD Michaels: Saving Laura
Lynn Michaels, Rescuing Kyle
Wren Michaels: The Fox & The Hound
Kat Mizera: Protecting Bobbi
Keira Montclair, Wolf and the Wild Scots
Mary B Moore: Force Protection

LeTeisha Newton: Protecting Butterfly
Angela Nicole: Protecting the Donna
MJ Nightingale: Protecting Beauty
Sarah O'Rourke: Saving Liberty
Victoria Paige: Reclaiming Izabel
Anne L. Parks: Mason
Debra Parmley: Protecting Pippa
Lainey Reese: Protecting New York
TL Reeve and Michele Ryan: Extracting Mateo
Elena M. Reyes: Keeping Ava
Angela Rush: Charlotte
Rose Smith: Saving Satin
Jenika Snow: Protecting Lily
Lynne St. James: SEAL's Spitfire
Dee Stewart: Conner
Harley Stone: Rescuing Mercy
Jen Talty: Burning Desire
Reina Torres, Rescuing Hi'ilani
Megan Vernon: Protecting Us

Police and Fire: Operation Alpha World

Freya Barker: Burning for Autumn
Julia Bright, Justice for Amber
Anna Brooks, Guarding Georgia
KaLyn Cooper: Justice for Gwen
Aspen Drake: Sheltering Emma
Deanndra Hall: Shelter for Sharla
Barb Han: Kace
EM Hayes: Gambling for Ashleigh

CM Steele: Guarding Hope
Reina Torres: Justice for Sloane
Aubree Valentine, Justice for Danielle
Stacey Wilk: Stage Fright

Tarpley VFD Series

Silver James, Fighting for Elena
Deanndra Hall, Fighting for Carly
Haven Rose, Fighting for Calliope
MJ Nightingale, Fighting for Jemma
TL Reeve, Fighting for Brittney
Nicole Flockton, Fighting for Nadia

As you know, this book included at least one character from Susan Stoker's books. To check out more, see below.

SEAL of Protection: Legacy Series

Securing Caite

Securing Brenae (novella)

Securing Sidney

Securing Piper

Securing Zoey

Securing Avery (May 2020)

Securing Kalee (Sept 2020)

Securing Jane (novella) (Feb 2021)

SEAL Team Hawaii Series

Finding Elodie (Apr 2021)

Finding Lexie (Aug 2021)

Finding Kenna (Oct 2021)

Finding Monica (TBA)

Finding Carly (TBA)

Finding Ashlyn (TBA)

Delta Team Two Series

Shielding Gillian

Shielding Kinley (Aug 2020)

Shielding Aspen (Oct 2020)

Shielding Riley (Jan 2021)

Shielding Devyn (TBA)

Shielding Ember (TBA)
Shielding Sierra (TBA)

Delta Force Heroes Series

Rescuing Rayne (FREE!)
Rescuing Aimee (novella)
Rescuing Emily
Rescuing Harley
Marrying Emily (novella)
Rescuing Kassie
Rescuing Bryn
Rescuing Casey
Rescuing Sadie (novella)
Rescuing Wendy
Rescuing Mary
Rescuing Macie (Novella)

Badge of Honor: Texas Heroes Series

Justice for Mackenzie (FREE!)
Justice for Mickie
Justice for Corrie
Justice for Laine (novella)
Shelter for Elizabeth
Justice for Boone
Shelter for Adeline
Shelter for Sophie
Justice for Erin
Justice for Milena

Shelter for Blythe
Justice for Hope
Shelter for Quinn
Shelter for Koren
Shelter for Penelope

SEAL of Protection Series

Protecting Caroline (FREE!)
Protecting Alabama
Protecting Fiona
Marrying Caroline (novella)
Protecting Summer
Protecting Cheyenne
Protecting Jessyka
Protecting Julie (novella)
Protecting Melody
Protecting the Future
Protecting Kiera (novella)
Protecting Alabama's Kids (novella)
Protecting Dakota

New York Times, USA Today and *Wall Street Journal* Bestselling Author Susan Stoker has a heart as big as the state of Tennessee where she lives, but this all American girl has also spent the last fourteen years living in Missouri, California, Colorado, Indiana, and Texas. She's married to a retired Army man who now gets to follow *her* around the country.

www.stokeraces.com
www.AcesPress.com
susan@stokeraces.com

Made in the USA
Columbia, SC
10 June 2020

10582549R00153